FRACTURED TRUST

COASTAL INVESTIGATION BOOK THREE

SHEILA KELL

Cunningham Publishing, USA

FRACTURED TRUST
Copyright © 2024 by Sheila Kell

All rights reserved.
Published by Cunningham Publishing

ISBN: 978-1-957587-08-0
E-ISBN: 978-1-957587-09-7

Printed in the United States of America

To my newest beta reader, Alisha Collins,
Thank you for your long-standing support.
I appreciate your natural talent and welcome you to
the team.

Titles by Sheila Kell

<u>Coastal Investigation Series</u>
Deadly Betrayal
Read Between the Lines
Fractured Trust

<u>HIS Series</u>
His Desire
His Choice
His Return
His Chance
His Destiny
His Family
His Heart
His Fantasy
Evening Shadows
Midnight Escape
A Hamilton Christmas
Afternoon Delight

"Sheila Kell is a mistress of the genre, and she has a gift for crafting well-rounded, rock-solid characters and scenes that are emotionally charged and interesting."
–Readers' Favorite

Chapter One

AS I STROLL through a vast chain department store, I glimpse a gray T-shirt titled "Nana is my name, and spoiling is my game." The feeling of loss in my heart deepens, leaving a gaping hole. Even though I am a Nana, I have never been called by that loving name. The sight of the shirt only adds to my misery, and I feel the urge to escape the clothing store and the painful emotions it brings.

Losing my only son was a devastating blow. In the aftermath, I feel a deep sense of emptiness, realizing that I may never experience the joy of a child calling me "Nana."

The thought of having a grandson fills me with joy, but this joy was taken away when his mother and the person claiming to be his father separated him from me and my son.

It took more than a decade before that manipulative bitch revealed the truth to my son—that he was the father. As a result, my son and I missed out on nearly eleven years with my grandson. How could a mother do such a thing to her own family? All because she favored one man over the other. It's a truly heart-wrenching and cruel situation.

The betrayal shattered the trust built over a lifetime between these two men, who had been inseparable best friends. It was shocking to see how my son's closest companion could betray him in such a way.

No one knows that my son told me the truth the night before he was murdered. I can't ignore his words.

"Momma, I have something to tell you, and it's both good and bad," my son said.

He would often say this when he was uncertain whether I would approve of the information he was about to share with me. "Go ahead with the good. We'll deal with the bad later."

"I have a son."

My heart leaped. I am a grandmother. It was what I wanted more than anything. "How old is he?"

"He's ten, but his mother lied and said someone else is the father."

As I reflected on the past, anger washed over me when I realized I had missed out on a decade of my grandson's life. My mind was troubled by questions about why my son had chosen to keep this information concealed from me. "Why didn't you tell me before today?"

"Because I hadn't known. Until now."

"Well, let's go get him." I was up and ready to head out the door immediately. I thought about what we needed to buy to please a ten-year-old boy. Football, video games, a dog....

"Sit, Momma. Here's the bad part. The mother told everyone else that the other man was the father. She only

told me last night, and now she's dead. She can't tell anyone else the truth."

At that time, I had no idea that my son was being accused of the woman's murder. Nevertheless, I continue to question the validity of the police's account. I am inclined to believe that this alleged father murdered her to suppress the truth.

As for the mother, I want to say, "God rest her soul," but I am so angry with her and her actions that I can't bring myself to bless her. The Christian in me is warring with what I want versus what I have.

Before my son was senselessly murdered, we carefully deliberated and concluded that the most prudent course of action would be to formally request a DNA test to initiate the process of establishing the biological paternity of the child. I was shattered when my beloved son fell victim to that fractured trust between friends.

The man who claimed to be the boy's father murdered my son to conceal the truth. Oh, my son's killer pled self-defense, but I know better. He didn't want to lose the boy. I refuse to believe the lies told by the police that my son was running guns. The imposter father was once a police officer, and they're sticking together to create a conspiracy to keep the boy away from his true family. The imposter father didn't want me to know I had a grandson.

Despite my efforts to find contentment in the knowledge that my grandson is alive and being well looked after, it's an ongoing struggle. The fact that he was taken from me at birth, unbeknownst to me at the time, continues to weigh heavily on my heart, making it difficult to find peace.

Because of the bitch and the imposter father, I missed the first time my grandson took a step. I wasn't there when he rode his first bike and skinned his knees. I have no Christmas or birthday photos of him where we celebrated together. I have nothing, and "he"—the imposter father—has it all: my grandson and the life stolen from me and my son.

Since my husband passed from a heart attack years ago, I have been wearying of the solitude, particularly now that I have learned about the presence of family. The young boy is my grandson. He is the physical embodiment of my DNA…my flesh and blood…and my sole living relative. He will be in my life, and I in his—legally or illegally.

I plan to start by taking legal action, including requesting a paternity test to establish the truth. Once we have the test results, this whole ordeal will end, and the boy can be with his actual family where he belongs.

I firmly believe that the imposter father will refuse to consent to undergo the suggested test. See, he knows the truth also and will fight me tooth and nail for the honor of being called "father." How do I know he knows? My son had carefully planned the momentous decision to confide in him. I firmly believe, deep in my heart, that my son managed to do so before drawing his final breath. It is inconceivable to me that he would leave this world with the truth untold.

In the event of a custody dispute, I will not hesitate to take my grandson and leave. I am determined to do whatever it takes to protect and be with what little remains of my son. No mother should have to endure the heartbreaking experience of losing a child repeatedly.

I am a grandmother. I want my grandson in my life. I am his only "true" living relative. He belongs with me, not the imposter father. Now, I feel like I'm perceived as an old crackpot clinging to remnants of her son. However, I am unwavering in my belief in the truth and determined to prove it.

I believe in the power of careful planning. I consider myself a master strategist, and I am aware of my grandson's summer plans. I am determined to find a way to be with him every day. My goal is to win his affection. If that fails, I am prepared to run with him if it becomes necessary. I refuse to let anyone take away what I believe is rightfully mine—absolutely no one.

I am Vincent St. Amant's mother, and Henry Kyle Walker is my grandson. I am determined to have him in my life regardless of any difficulties or obstacles that may arise.

Chapter Two

"HENRY KYLE," JD Walker called out to his son in the next room. "Why did you pack only one pair of underwear for a two-week trip?" JD should have anticipated the repercussions of entrusting his ten-year-old son with packing for summer camp. Despite his hopeful expectations, it turned out that the boy wasn't quite prepared to make appropriate choices, especially when selecting suitable clothing for the trip.

Thankfully, JD had the foresight to check the bag, which turned out to be crucial. Removing Lucy, the cat, from the top of the duffel, he exchanged Henry Kyle's clothing. JD had his son repacked in no time. He'd considered taking out the headphones so his son would be required to socialize. Still, he thought other children might bring their headphones, as it was now trendy, and he didn't want his son to feel excluded.

JD checked his watch and restrained himself from cursing. He had worked hard to control his language for the sake of his son, and he wouldn't let Henry Kyle down now, even if they were running late.

Eagerly, JD picked up Henry Kyle's new duffel bag and swiftly strode into the warm, inviting kitchen. There, he found Cassie, his devoted fiancée, serving breakfast. Homemade blueberry pancakes were her specialty. Before they married, he hoped she learned her mother's divine cinnamon roll recipe.

"Breakfast is ready." She leaned in to kiss him.

To his great disappointment, he hastily ended the kiss. "No time."

"Dad, do you promise to feed Cooper and Lucy every day while I'm gone? And make sure they have water? Oh, and you have to clean their litter boxes, too."

He grimaced. *Great. The litterboxes.* That is precisely why JD hadn't considered a cat. But he guessed it'd be that or scooping poop from the backyard. Maybe he'd get an automated litter box while his son was at camp. "No problem."

Cassie gestured to the kitchen table. "Sit for breakfast."

JD reached across the table and selected a fluffy pancake from the piled plate, savoring its aroma. He took a big bite, attempting to disregard Cassie's scrutinizing expression. "We're late." He hastily consumed the dry breakfast while on the move, longing for a drizzle of syrup to enhance the flavor.

Cassie swiftly cleared the area, wiping surfaces and neatly stacking the dishes in the dishwasher while JD and Henry Kyle worked together to load the car. JD knew it was time to discuss certain things with his son since things happened at summer camp. His mind warred with his heart because his son was only eleven, but he'd wanted to kiss Cassie that young.

JD cleared his throat and leaned against his truck, ready to tackle "the talk." "Henry Kyle."

"Yeah, Dad?"

"We need to talk."

Henry Kyle looked put out but stood waiting. "Okay."

"It's about boys and girls and things that can happen at summer camp."

His son's face turned bright red. "Dad, please, no."

JD didn't slow down. He had put in extensive preparation to ensure he would get this right. "At summer camp, things happen—"

"Dad, please stop."

"No, you're old enough to hear this."

"Dad, please. I'm not going to have sex at summer camp."

Narrowing his eyes, JD wondered just how much his son had picked up from attending Cassie's Mom's homeschool. He couldn't help but question whether his son's friends in the neighborhood were also sharing insights about the birds and the bees.

"Okay." JD paused briefly. "But you may want to kiss a girl."

Henry Kyle slumped his shoulders. "I've already kissed a girl."

JD straightened. He had hoped his son would wait a bit longer, but they had to grow up eventually. "Who?"

Henry Kyle scuffed a foot over the white gravel lining the paved driveway. "Amelia Brighton."

JD racked his brain, trying to recall the girls' names in the neighborhood as he scrolled through his mental files. He believed her father was a criminal, so that wouldn't work. He cleared his throat. "About Amelia—"

His son cut him off again. Henry Kyle's despondent expression tugged at JD's heartstrings. How could he find the words to explain to his son that he couldn't spend time with this girl? Memories flooded back the anguish he experienced when his father forbade him from pursuing anything that brought him joy, especially spending time with Cassie.

"Don't worry. I found out Amelia kissed Gary and Ray, also. She was trying to find out who kissed the best."

Okay. The unexpected turn of events took JD aback. Although uncertain, he was intrigued enough to ask about it. "And?"

"She said it was me, but I didn't like that she did that, so I'm not having anything to do with her again."

JD found it reassuring that the situation prevented him from having a potentially challenging discussion if Henry Kyle were to fall in love with Amelia. His proud papa's stance of shoulders back and chest puffed out also came into play, with his son being the best kisser of the boys. It wasn't something he should be proud of, but he was. Men absolutely enjoyed the craziest of things.

"Well, be careful out there. There are diseases—"

"Ew, Dad. I know. Miss Pat discussed them in health class."

Perhaps JD ought to devote more attention to his son's homework. On the other hand, he felt grateful to Pat for sparing him from having a difficult conversation. "What did this class entail?" Maybe he'd be off the hook entirely because he remained uncertain about how to broach the subjects of sex, condoms, and the potential consequences of fleeting encounters, especially given how brief they generally are at Henry Kyle's age.

JD's stomach twisted into knots as he grappled with the realization that kids were engaging in sexual activity at such a young age. He vividly recalled reading the troubling statistics while preparing for the difficult conversation with his son. JD desperately hoped his son would exercise caution and wait until he found the right partner. However, he was acutely aware that he couldn't impose his will on his son's choices.

"Everything, Dad. You don't need to look so pale. I'm not going to have sex yet. I don't even know a girl I'd want to have sex with."

Well, that relieved JD. Mostly. "And Amelia?"

Henry Kyle sighed. "She lost her chance for me even to hold her hand."

JD inwardly smiled. "Well, you can always talk to me about this." JD hesitated, unsure if he could manage any forthcoming conversations, but he remained receptive to the idea of listening.

"Uh, okay, Dad. Can we talk about something else?"

JD felt the urge to burst into laughter. He pushed himself off the back of the truck and strolled to the side, subtly signaling to Cassie that it was safe for her to come outside. "Sure, champ. Are you excited about summer camp?"

Cassie rushed down the steps, her smile filled with cautious optimism. As she reached the bottom, she arched her eyebrows inquisitively, silently conveying her desire to know how the conversation had unfolded. JD, uncertain of the outcome himself, responded with a tentative nod, hoping to provide her with the information she sought. All he knew was that his son wouldn't have sex at this tender age.

"I'm excited. Do you know they have a zipline? I can't wait to ride it."

JD couldn't help but envision his son experiencing the exhilaration of adventurous activities. Following his thrilling parasailing experience, his son developed a keen interest in adrenaline-inducing sports and even expressed curiosity about skydiving. JD recalled his desire to skydive as a kid. Now? He wasn't so sure.

Cassie gracefully extended her arm, offering a small, neatly folded paper bag to Henry Kyle with a warm smile. "I packed you a sandwich in case you don't get to eat until later today."

His son has willingly accepted it. "Thank you, Miss Cassie. My tummy thanks you." Henry Kyle stuffed the bag in his backpack.

JD felt a surge of pride as he watched his son express gratitude to Cassie. He knew that the sandwich would disappear in mere minutes.

"Are we ready to get on the road?" JD inquired.

"Let's go." Henry Kyle whooped.

"Jump in." JD held the front passenger door open for Cassie. Vivid memories of his first kiss with her flooded his mind. He cherished the moment, though he wouldn't confess to his son that he had swiped a kiss at the same age. It had been nothing more than a swift, innocent peck—no lingering embrace or intertwining of tongues.

As everyone loaded into the truck, JD reached over and turned on the air conditioner, feeling a pang of regret that he hadn't pre-cooled the truck. The relentless heat of Gulf Islands was becoming increasingly unbearable.

"Should we sing camp songs?" JD glanced behind him as he backed out of the driveway.

"Please, no, Dad."

JD and Cassie gazed at each other, sharing a smile. They adored JD's son but were eager for two weeks of uninterrupted nights together without the subsequent morning awkwardness.

"Okay, champ. We'll play it your way." JD adjusted the radio station to the old-school alternative and increased the volume, knowing his son preferred it. He could tolerate the music for that brief period since his son could experience something JD had never had the chance to do—enjoy a summer camp like all his friends had when they were growing up.

He found himself reflecting on memories of his friends, and a particular conversation with Vince came to mind. Feeling uncertain about his next steps, he grappled with the decision of whether to pursue a DNA test. Additionally, he pondered over the prospect of informing Henry Kyle that there might be a possibility he is not his biological son. Adding to the situation's complexity, he questioned whether Henry Kyle was emotionally mature enough to understand the circumstances.

JD's confidence in his unbreakable bond with his son was unwavering, regardless of Henry Kyle's biological origins. To JD, Henry Kyle was his son in every sense of the word, and nothing could alter that conviction. When JD received a mysterious note bearing the words, "I know the truth," he was left bewildered, yet a deep intuition told him that it was connected to Henry Kyle.

He was being persistently harassed and resolute in his refusal to tolerate such behavior. Henry Kyle was his son—that's the end of the story.

Chapter Three

CASSIE COULDN'T BELIEVE her luck—her mom and Henry Kyle were out of town, and there was no case to work on. It was just her and JD. After much consideration, she decided this was the appropriate time to reach an agreement on a date for their long-awaited wedding. JD had been hesitant, but Cassie was eager to take the next step in their relationship.

As they were returning from New Orleans and had just dropped off Henry Kyle at summer camp, Cassie broached a new topic for discussion. "What do you think about getting married in November?"

Cassie dreamt of a picturesque beach wedding with the soothing sound of waves and the sun's warmth. However, she couldn't shake off her worries about November's strong, cold winds and the looming threat of hurricanes. Despite these concerns, she was determined to find the perfect location for their special day within the next six months. The central area of Coastal Investigation held a special place in her heart, as it was the exact spot where she and JD had once rekindled their love, making it an ideal backup venue for their wedding.

The memory of that meeting came flooding back. It was a painful, tense experience. JD had wrongly accused her of obtaining a restraining order against him when he left for college, an entirely untrue claim. It was later discovered that JD's father had deceived him, weaving a web of lies to shatter JD's happiness, fracturing the trust between father and son.

She reminded herself of the numerous obstacles they had overcome to reach this point. Years of being apart, a father's attempt to separate them, and interference from past partners had all been in vain. There were so many lost years to make up for, and she was determined not to wait any longer to become JD's wife.

JD glanced at her before returning his eyes to the road. "November is a nice month."

"JD," she said, turning fully to him, "this is important. We need to set a date."

He heaved a heavy sigh and steered the truck toward the shoulder of the highway. JD gradually decreased the truck's speed as other cars zoomed past, eventually stopping safely on the roadside. Turning towards the passenger seat, JD let out another sigh. "Okay, let's do this."

"You make it sound like a death sentence. I thought you wanted to get married." Her anxiety increased to a higher level, causing her heart to race and her mind to become overwhelmed with worry and fear.

"I do."

"Well, let's set a date. I'm tired of running home to change or not wanting Henry Kyle to see me staying over."

JD casually propped his arm on the steering wheel and gazed out the front window.

Her heart felt like it was stuck in her throat as she grappled with the possibility that he might be trying to appease her. It was almost unbelievable to her that this nerve-wracking discussion could actually be taking place. "I– I thought you wanted to get married."

He turned to her. "I do, but—"

She awaited his next words with a pounding heart, but he stayed silent, shrouding her in dread as the realization dawned upon her. Was he about to end their relationship? How could this be unfolding? They had always been a perfect match, so what had precipitated this change in him? Was the concept of marriage terrifying him? After all, he had never married Henry Kyle's mother. Perhaps he harbored a fear of commitment, a common affliction for some men.

JD gently removed his hand from the steering wheel and tenderly grasped her hand, locking eyes with her in a moment of connection. "Cassie, I love you. I don't want to marry you in November."

Tears welled up in her eyes, her heart aching at his words. Now, faced with this revelation, she pondered her next move. Should she plead with him or choose another path?

"I want to marry you as soon as possible."

Cassie was astonished and relieved as tears of joy slid down her face. "I'd like that."

With his thumb, he wiped away a tear. "Don't cry, sweetheart. If you want to wait until November, we will."

She playfully swatted at his broad chest. "No, you dolt, I want to marry you now."

"Well then, can we pull this shindig together in two weeks and for when Patricia and Henry Kyle return?"

She felt a sudden wave of panic. Only two weeks? The thought was to wear her mother's dress from when Patricia married Cassie's father. But how long would it take for alterations? If it was going to be a beach wedding —an idea she favored—she realized there wasn't much time to bring everything together.

"Yes," she smiled. "On the beach in two weeks." Then she pondered their most pressing challenge. "Who will marry us?"

JD shrugged. "Nan."

"Nan?" That threw her. "Is she, by chance, licensed to officiate marriages?"

He nodded. "She is."

"I like the idea. Okay, Nan will marry us in two weeks." Her heart swelled with an overwhelming joy that bubbled inside her, almost on the verge of bursting. At long last, they would be united as husband and wife. This had been her cherished dream since she first met him on the school bus during elementary school.

"Good. That's settled." JD maneuvered the steering wheel, signaling with his blinker as he prepared to merge back onto the bustling highway. A timely break in traffic presented itself, allowing them to rejoin the flow of vehicles seamlessly.

Cassie hesitated to press her luck, but the matter demanded deeper discussion. She felt a bit lost without her mother by her side to brainstorm. "Now, we need a location on the beach."

"I already have one."

JD's statement caught her off guard. While she had contemplated it, she had yet to discover a venue that truly resonated with her for her wedding day.

"It's the place I proposed to you. I love that location on the beach."

The place held a special significance for her because it was where he had proposed to her. She cherished the memory of that moment and felt a deep connection to the location because of it. "How large do you want the wedding to be? I mean, guests?"

JD took a moment before answering. She was glad he considered it instead of just "leaving it to the woman to decide," like so many men she knew.

"I was thinking just family. Henry Kyle, Patricia, Gus, and Nan."

"And Daisy." Since working for the agency, Cassie and the assistant have managed to mend their initial conflict and develop a friendly relationship.

"And Daisy." He glanced at her and laughed. "We definitely shouldn't forget her."

Cassie felt like she was sitting on cloud nine when they finally agreed to the wedding. Everything in her life felt idyllic, but then a sudden thought struck her. "Oh no!"

"What's wrong?"

She bit her lip before responding, "Levi. I want him to give me away. I'm not sure he can be here with such short notice."

JD shrugged. "Call him. If he can't, we'll adjust. Besides, wasn't he due to start with CI soon?"

Gracious, she had the perfect man. She pulled her phone from her purse and selected Levi from her contacts. "Yes, but I thought that was next month." When Levi answered her call, she couldn't hold back her excitement. "We're getting married in two weeks. Can you be here?"

JD laughed, but Cassie was too captivated by her joy to pay it any mind.

"Kiddo, I'll be there with bells on." Levi's voice projected joy as he spoke, conveying his happiness effortlessly. She cherished him deeply and hoped that her mother and Levi would find their way to each other.

"Thank—"

A massive force from the left struck the truck, violently jerking it into a sharp turn and then a spinning motion. In the chaos, Cassie's grip on the phone faltered as she desperately clutched the door and dashboard to steady herself.

As the airbags forcefully inflated with a loud whooshing sound, JD's grip on the steering wheel slackened, and the vehicle careened out of control. The vehicle skidded, flipped, and rolled over multiple times, causing her to be thrown against the side airbag or the middle of the truck with each chaotic rotation. The vehicle finally stopped, tipping over onto the driver's side with a loud thud. The air was filled with the unsettling sounds of metal groaning and glass crunching.

Panic and excruciating pain completely overwhelmed her as she struggled to process the rapid sequence of events that had just unfolded. She was left bewildered, desperately trying to grasp the exact nature of what had transpired.

Cassie fought against the force of the deflating airbag as it rapidly retreated from the dashboard. She could hear brakes screeching in her subconscious as cars abruptly stopped and people shouted. But with her head hurting and her vision tunneling, she could only see the blood on an unconscious JD's head before her vision narrowed to black.

Chapter Four

AGONIZING PAIN SHOT through Cassie, causing her to emit a low, guttural groan.

"Oh, good. You're awake." The unfamiliar male voice shattered her sleep, jolting her fully awake with a sense of unease.

Looking around, she swiftly discerned that she was in a hospital. Puzzled by her surroundings, she turned to her visitor with curiosity. "Levi?"

"Hey, kiddo. You gave me quite a scare."

"How? What?" Her foggy mind couldn't comprehend what had transpired. She had been in the truck with JD, conversing with Levi, and—

The overwhelming sense of panic began to well up inside her, growing stronger with each passing moment. "JD?"

Levi reached out and softly patted her hand, offering a comforting and reassuring gesture. "Shh, settle yourself."

"Wait. How are you here? I was just speaking with you." Hadn't she been? Hadn't she been asking him to escort her down the aisle?

"Someone picked up the phone you'd been using and relayed what had happened. I jumped the next flight to Gulfport."

She could not comprehend or make sense of that information now. "JD?" Why did Levi deliberately avoid addressing her question the first time? She fervently hoped that JD wouldn't sustain serious injuries or— She couldn't bring herself to contemplate the alternative.

"Like you, he's in ICU. It's the room next to yours."

"I need to see him." Cassie struggled to sit up, but as she attempted to do so, she faltered, holding her head in agony. The tape and IV in her hand tugged at her tender skin, causing further discomfort.

Levi gently touched her shoulder with tenderness and concern, halting her movement. "No. First, you allow the doctor to examine you while you're awake. Let me go round her up."

After Levi exited the cramped, brightly lit room, Cassie made another attempt to rise from the bed. With great effort, she managed to sit up and dangle her feet over the edge, but a sudden wave of dizziness and the appearance of spots before her eyes stopped her. As her vision narrowed to a tunnel, she reluctantly acknowledged that she didn't have the strength to continue.

Returning with someone Cassie guessed was a nurse, Levi smiled. "We're lucky. The doctor is on the floor doing rounds. She'll be here shortly."

"Whoa there." The male nurse quickly and urgently made his way to her side.

Levi moved to her opposite side and gently grasped her hand. "Come on, kiddo. You had a head injury. You can't just jump up like this."

After a brief knock sounded, Cassie glanced upward and caught sight of a diminutive woman clad in a lab coat, who couldn't have been more than twenty, as she entered the room. Cassie was skeptical that such a youthful individual could be a doctor.

"Hi, I'm Doctor Myers." So, the kid was her doctor—just great. "He's right. You shouldn't try to stand just yet. Let me examine you. Then we'll take it in small steps to get you back on your feet as quickly as possible."

Cassie's eyebrow arched in response to the pronouncement.

Dr. Myers smiled. "I get that a lot. Believe me. I'm a lot older than I look."

The nurse offered a warm and comforting smile. "You're in great hands." He then departed the room, leaving her alone with a child doctor.

"JD?" She felt exhausted from having to repeat herself constantly. The extent of his injuries was shrouded in silence, and this filled her with a gripping fear that she couldn't shake until she obtained some answers.

Dr. Myers glanced up from the tablet she had been fervently scrolling through, her eyes momentarily filled with concentration before meeting Cassie's gaze. "How do you feel sitting up?"

"Feeling a bit dizzy," she confessed as she struggled to keep her balance. The urge to see JD was overwhelming. She'd have said anything to escape the confines of the hospital and its medical staff if it meant moving closer to reuniting with him.

"Okay, I'll examine you like this then." Dr. Myers removed the stethoscope from her neck, placed the probes in her ears, and listened to Cassie's heart. "As for Mr. Walker, he's not doing as well as you."

Cassie felt a sudden jolt in her heart as she contemplated the implication. She couldn't help but wonder how bad she must be if JD was considered worse.

"Whoa! Take a moment to calm down. Your heart rate has suddenly shot up, so trying to relax is important."

Cassie closed her eyes, trying to steady her racing heart as the doctor had suggested. Yet, it was incredibly challenging to find peace, especially knowing that JD was injured, and she could not be by his side immediately.

"If you check out okay, I'll get a wheelchair, and Mr. Levi can bring you to Mr. Walker's room to visit."

"We're not family yet." Cassie knew the rules for the ICU. Wait, how did Levi get back?

"Ah, I see. Your father has informed me that you are to be married to Mr. Walker. In light of this, we'll make an exception in this case."

Cassie glanced at Levi, who was standing just behind the doctor. Her father, huh?

Levi nonchalantly raised his shoulders and flashed her a shy, apologetic smile.

After enduring a thorough examination that required her to follow the doctor's finger, Cassie's impatience was palpable. She felt a strong urge to push the young physician aside and personally check on JD, even if it meant crawling to his side.

"Your scans and x-rays are good. You have a severe concussion, and since you were out for almost twenty-four hours, we'd like to keep you overnight once more, just to be safe. You've also got bruises where the seat belt held you, slight burns on your arms and chest from the airbag, and cuts from flying glass, so those will give you some pain, but they're not serious. I'll prescribe something mild for it."

Cassie was not bothered by anything if she could see JD. "May I see JD now?"

Dr. Myers smiled with a kind and genuine expression. "Okay. Let me get a nurse to bring a wheelchair, and we'll let you see him."

"Is it serious?" Cassie was utterly overwhelmed by worry, unable to shake free from its suffocating grip.

"Yes." Dr. Myers grimaced, her brows furrowing as if in pain. "He's had a TBI. We've placed him in a medically induced coma due to swelling on his brain that concerns us. We're working on bringing the swelling down."

In a sudden, heart-wrenching moment, Cassie watched as her idyllic world unraveled before her eyes. The mere thought of losing JD was unbearable—simply inconceivable—especially after the arduous journey they had endured to find their way back to each other. Their wedding day loomed just two weeks away, and the idea of him not being okay was unfathomable.

"Please just take me to him." As she spoke in a demanding tone, regret washed over her. Nevertheless, seeing JD was an urgent priority for her.

As Dr. Myers approached the door, she suddenly pivoted around with speed and urgency. "Oh, the nurse mentioned that when Mr. Walker arrived, he mumbled about cats. Does he have pets?"

Cassie nodded—her immediate regret was palpable as searing pain exploded through her head. She braced herself, unable to support the weight of her head with her hands, fearing that the doctor would deny her permission to leave her bed.

"Do we need to send out the local rescue group to care for them?"

Cassie was disheartened to learn from the statement that the hospital planned to keep JD longer than she was comfortable with. "No. He's got a son." Oh God. Henry Kyle! He'd be alone at home. No, wait—he was at summer camp.

She sat there, battling confusion, her hand resting on her forehead as she rubbed it in frustration. Suddenly, a glimmer of a solution crossed her mind—she could ask her mother for help. But then she remembered that her mother was still out of town. Frustrated and lost, she dropped her hand and glanced at Levi pleadingly.

With a gentle, genuine smile that reached his eyes, Levi expressed his agreement by nodding slowly. "I've got it." He turned to the doctor. "We'll get them fed and cared for."

Cassie tried to calm her nerves, although she was still filled with a sense of urgency to see her fiancé. The desire to send the doctor away so she could grab a wheelchair was overwhelming. Despite her intense yearning to be by JD's side, Cassie was acutely aware that she could not walk to him, a realization she had to admit to herself.

Dr. Myers assured her, "I'll have the nurse come right in," before exiting the room.

Cassie gazed intently at Levi and asked with a hint of urgency, "Just how serious is the situation?"

"He's not doing well. In addition to a broken left arm, he also had a dislocated left shoulder, which has been treated. However, he'll experience significant pain when he wakes up."

Her heart raced as she asked, "The swelling?" Raw terror took hold of her, the thought crossing her mind: Didn't people die from that?

Levi gently lifted his hand to readjust her hospital gown, carefully drawing it back over her shoulder as it had slipped down her arm. "It's not good, but he's got a great team here." He dropped into the small, worn armchair next to the bed.

"Oh, God."

"JD was not as lucky as you were. His side airbag failed to deploy, resulting in a major impact when the truck jolted and settled on the driver's side."

Cassie felt the sting of tears as she instinctively closed her eyes, allowing the memories to flood back. She could vividly recall the deafening impact of the vehicle colliding with theirs, the disorienting sensation of the ensuing spin, and the harrowing moment of weightlessness when the truck flipped, and she found herself suspended upside down, held in place by her seat belt. Every detail seemed etched into her memory, as if time had slowed to a crawl during the traumatic event.

Levi cleared his throat before asking, "While we're waiting, can you recall what happened?"

In a reflective pause, Cassie vividly recounted the harrowing experience. "Suddenly, another vehicle attempted to merge into our lane or swerved into it, forcing us into a sharp turn and then a spin. The next thing I knew, we were flipping over, but I couldn't comprehend why it happened."

"Hmm."

Levi's one-word response puzzled her. She couldn't quite interpret his meaning. "Hmm, what?"

Levi casually raised his hand as a gesture of dismissal and calmly stated, "Nothing."

Once again, just one word seemed to push her buttons. With a firm tone, she insisted, "It's obvious there's something on your mind. Please, share it with me."

Levi heaved a wary sigh, the exhale trembling slightly as his eyes met hers. "Based on what happened, there are two potential scenarios. First, it's possible that the side airbag was faulty and didn't function properly during the incident. In this case, you may have grounds to take legal action against the truck manufacturer to seek coverage for your medical expenses and potentially more."

"Understood. I see your point, but I'd rather shift our focus to something else. My primary concern is for JD's recovery."

Cassie glanced at the door, and her eyes met the comforting warmth of the nurse's smile, which immediately put her at ease. "It's so great to see you awake. Let me take you to your man," the nurse said kindly. With the nurse's help, Cassie settled into the wheelchair, clutching her gown tightly to ensure her privacy. As the nurse pushed the wheelchair, Cassie took in the sights and sounds of the ICU room.

She felt her heart plummet in her chest, a sinking sensation threatening to overpower her. Tears welled in her eyes as she surveyed the array of machines in the room, each connected to JD somehow. The rhythmic beeping and whirring sounds filled the space, emphasizing the stark contrast between his fragile state and the sterile hospital environment. It was clear that JD was entirely reliant on the machines for his vital functions, unable to breathe on his own. A suffocating sense of fear gripped Cassie as she grappled with the overwhelming helplessness of the situation.

The nurse stopped by JD's bedside and secured the chair's wheels to prevent unexpected movement. "I'll return in an hour unless you call me sooner," she reassured.

Cassie's head swam as she nodded, trying to clear her vision. She focused on JD and grasped his hand, leaning over his belly. "Honey, you need to wake up," she pleaded as tears slipped down her cheeks.

"I'll just leave you."

Cassie was unaware of whether Levi had left the room. Her attention was solely on JD. She quickly sat upright but composed herself before speaking. "One moment. You mentioned that one of two things had happened. Would you please elaborate on the second thing?"

Levi let out a deep, weary sigh before giving his response. "Or perhaps someone tampered with it," he suggested.

Chapter Five

I IDENTIFIED MYSELF as family and phoned the hospital to inquire about JD Walker's health. I was left in absolute uncertainty about whether he had managed to survive the accident. Someone informed me that he was in the Intensive Care Unit, but his fiancée was conscious and alert. Surprisingly, she'd been in the truck dropping my grandson at summer camp. Oh well.

I took a leap of faith by inviting Henry Kyle to attend this particular camp, and I'm delighted that both he and JD accepted the invitation. I look forward to spending quality time with my grandson daily for the next two weeks. I plan to wait until he feels at ease around me before revealing that I'm his grandmother. If the situation escalates to a legal battle, I'm confident he'll choose to come live with me. My financial well-being would allow me to fulfill his every wish, something his imposter father, who is a murderer, cannot provide.

I've been attempting to obtain custody of Henry Kyle without anyone knowing. Still, a recent legal consultation revealed that I don't have sufficient legal grounds to pursue this course of action. Since the boy's mother and biological father have both passed away, and no one else is aware of the child's parentage, this situation appears hopeless. Despite the challenges, I am determined and actively seeking legal representation to secure custody of Henry Kyle. My ultimate goal is to resolve this matter without resorting to court proceedings.

Henry Kyle is a delightful and well-mannered young boy who often lights up the room with his radiant smile. Although I have not been with him, I sincerely hope he has grown up in a loving and supportive home environment.

I stand at the base of the zipline, watching as my young grandson takes off. His excited shout of "Whoo Hoo" echoes as he zips along. His laughter is infectious and fills me with joy, mainly because he is my only remaining family. The bond I share with this child is incredibly special to me, and it pains me to have missed out on so many precious moments with him. Despite this, I'm thankful for our time together, even though he remains unaware of my role as his grandmother.

With a wide grin on his face, Henry Kyle eagerly approached me. "Mrs. Davis, did you see me?"

I wanted to ensure I could get the job at the camp without any issues, so I used a fake name just in case JD decided to check who would be on the employee/volunteer list. Fortunately, my neighbor and I bear a striking resemblance, so I could use her name and information without raising any suspicion. It proved effortless to obtain what I required from her. It's advisable for individuals to carefully shred their bills and bank statements before discarding them and avoid ordering their driver's license renewal via mail.

I responded with a beaming smile. "Are you planning to go again? There's still plenty of time for it."

"Is it okay for me to?" he asked with wide, hopeful eyes.

Although I don't know him personally, I can't help but feel a deep affection for this boy. There's something about him that reminds me of my son. Perhaps it's his jawline and cheekbones. However, when I look into his eyes, I can't help but see a resemblance to his bitch of a mother.

If Henry Kyle's mother were alive, I could kill the woman for her lies and running. For ten long years, she prevented me from seeing my grandson. Almost eleven years! I find this utterly unforgivable.

"Yes, you can." My hand extends, touching his perspiration-dampened shoulder, covered by a T-shirt. It's the first time I've reached out. Despite the rules prohibiting employees and volunteers from physical contact with the children, I find it difficult to resist. I yearn for this deeper connection.

Wordlessly, he dashes off to join the queue again. I observe him animatedly conversing with two other boys, presumably sharing their excitement about experiencing the zipline for the first time.

I'm looking forward to our upcoming boating and rafting adventure in just a few days. I'm excited to volunteer on Henry Kyle's boat and can't wait to experience the thrill of being on the water. When I altered the schedule to fulfill my longing to be near him, no one appeared to catch on.

As the eldest member of the volunteer team, I've taken on the role of head volunteer, which puts me in charge of overseeing all aspects of our projects and activities. The individual who put together the boat schedule was unaware of my need to be present with my grandson every day and at every event.

As I turned toward the person calling my name, I pondered my next steps regarding JD. It's a pity the accident didn't kill him. It was a gamble that couldn't be avoided. Nevertheless, there's still a glimmer of hope that he might not pull through due to the severity of his injuries.

Except for yesterday's accident, I'm determined to avoid any involvement in violence. Still, if I can't legally bring Henry Kyle home through proper channels, I may be forced to consider alternative, potentially illegal, methods. It would be most favorable if JD isn't an obstacle. I must explore alternative means to remove him.

I can't say that I employ a team of individuals who are capable of committing murder. I've heard that it's theoretically possible to illicitly gain access to a hospital and cause harm to a patient. However, this would only be achievable if I encountered someone within the hospital environment who lacks ethical standards. Fortunately, I have some time to plan my next steps because he is currently in a coma. I hope he remains in this state for over two weeks so that Henry Kyle and I can leave without trouble.

"Is there something I can help you with?" I raise an eyebrow inquisitively at the young volunteer, my curiosity piqued. Why are teenagers overseeing these children instead of their parents and grandparents who should be the primary protectors? Children who may become overwhelmed if another child gets sick should not be in charge.

"I'm curious about the changes in the boat schedule."

So, Kerry did notice. Well, too damn bad. "I decided to take the most rambunctious group so you wouldn't have to deal with them."

Kerry nods. "Okay. However, I don't mind."

I find it frustrating when children talk back or fail to follow instructions. Young people need to show respect for their elders. "It's done." I turn and walk away. This volunteer might be problematic, requiring close supervision. I can't draw attention from Kerry to Henry Kyle.

What can I do at camp, though? I cannot get my hands dirty because I can't go to jail. Then, I would never see my grandson.

JD is responsible for the death of my son, and he insists it was in self-defense. However, I am deeply skeptical of his claim. He will definitely pay for what he did, one way or another. He will either lose his own life or his son, Henry Kyle. I'm determined to ensure justice is served.

Don't mess with a grandma who knows what's best for her grandchild.

Chapter Six

"I UNDERSTAND," RESPONDED the camp counselor as Cassie provided details about JD's medical condition. Cassie fought hard to suppress her tears as she recounted the story, but she managed to compose herself for the sake of both JD and Henry Kyle.

"I thought I would pick up Henry Kyle and bring him home."

After a prolonged silence, just as Cassie began to think that the lady wouldn't say anything, Mrs. Davis sighed deeply. "I don't think that's wise. Henry Kyle can do nothing for his father. Here, he can be a kid and enjoy himself until he must deal with his father's condition. Besides, only a relative can pick him up, and you admitted you aren't one."

That made sense. However, because she had never experienced parenthood, she had to figure out how to handle the situation. She wondered what JD would do if he were in her shoes. Maybe she should allow Henry Kyle to enjoy being a child and refrain from stressing about it when there is nothing he can do. If JD's condition deteriorates, she will reassess and look for alternative ways to navigate the rules.

Cassie quietly nodded in agreement, although the camp counselor could not see her gesture. "I think that's a wise idea. I appreciate your counsel. Please take care of Henry Kyle for us."

"Oh, dearie, he's like family here."

"Thank you, Mrs. Davis." After concluding the call, Cassie shifted her attention to Levi, turning to face him directly. "The head volunteer says Henry Kyle is having a ball."

Levi carefully folded the newspaper and set it down on the sofa. He had been engrossed in the latest headlines while visiting Cassie's mom's home. "Is that why you chose not to tell him of his father's condition?"

Yes. No. Cassie had no idea why she'd chosen that route. "I think he's too young to understand completely. Besides, all he can do is sit by his dad's bedside. That's no place for a kid. Camp is better."

With a nod, Levi rose from his seat and raised his arms above his body, stretching them to both sides. "I agree."

Cassie couldn't help but admire Levi's physique. It wasn't in a romantic way, but more in a way that made her think he would make a great partner for her mom. Despite being an older man, he consistently maintained good physical fitness. While he didn't have defined six-pack abs, he also didn't have a noticeable stomach bulge. Cassie felt that her mom should think about getting to know the man better and perhaps start a relationship with him. Cassie realized she might have to devise a plan to help make this happen.

"Mom is coming home tonight."

"Oh yeah?" Levi arched an eyebrow. "Did you tell her about the accident and subsequent hospitalization?"

Of course, she had. Cassie had initially resisted the urge to disrupt her mother's much-needed mini-vacation, but her concern couldn't be stifled, resulting in her mother returning home earlier than expected. In the meantime, she planned to use her charm and persuasion to win Levi over and gain his support for her mother's benefit. "What do you think about her?" Cassie idly spun a pen adorned with the hospital's name between her fingers, lost in thought.

"I think she's nice and raised a wonderful daughter."

Cassie tilted her head to the side, her eyes narrowing in curiosity. "No, what do you really think of her?"

Levi reddened. He actually reddened. There was an unmistakable spark emanating from him. Cassie celebrated her success by mentally giving herself a high-five, feeling a sense of accomplishment and pride. She longed to welcome Levi into the family with open arms. Throughout the years, he had consistently been a source of kindness and had filled the void of the father figure she had yearned for.

"I– Uh," Levi stammered, "I think she's great. There. Is that what you wanted to hear?"

Cassie's fingers opened, releasing the pen, and her face lit up with a broad and joyful smile. "So, what are you going to do about it?" Soon, Levi will be relocating to the serene Gulf Islands and joining Coastal Investigation. As a result, she anticipated the opportunity to interact with him almost daily.

She wondered how her mom and Levi would get together, knowing her mom was fond of him. Levi and Patricia hadn't been on formal dates. However, they cherished the moments whenever he visited by taking leisurely walks after dinner. Now, he would be living in the same area, allowing Cassie to spend more time bringing them together.

"Don't you need to go lie down or something? The doctor said you still need watching." Levi promptly steered the conversation toward Cassie rather than her mother.

Cassie let out a light, amused chuckle as she playfully wagged her finger in Levi's direction. "You don't fool me, mister."

"All right, kiddo. That's enough of my love life or lack thereof. It's time you got some rest. Visiting hours start again soon at the ICU, and I know you want to be there."

Upon her discharge from the hospital, she found it challenging. When she was admitted, she could constantly stay beside JD's bedside. However, now that she was no longer a patient, she could only see him during designated visiting hours.

As Cassie reached for the pen, a wave of fear tightened its grip on her insides, sending a shiver down her spine. "Levi, what did you mean about tampering with JD's airbag? Do you think that's what happened?"

"Kiddo, I don't know. It's just a possibility. I wouldn't worry about it, though, because it's improbable that it happened. It's more likely the airbag failed to deploy due to a malfunction. I'd sue the crap out of the manufacturer, the dealer, and everyone in between."

Cassie didn't let thoughts of lawsuits or wealth cloud her mind. She was focused entirely on one thing: getting JD out of the hospital and making sure that he was safe.

Who would want to kill him? Could it have been someone he had arrested as a police detective?

"Stop going down that rabbit hole. I should never have said such a thing." Levi stood beside her, holding a glass of water and a pill, ready to offer her the medication. 'Here, take this like a good patient and lie down.'

Knowing Levi wouldn't discuss the possibility of foul play, Cassie followed his instructions, swallowing the terrible-tasting pill before heading to her room. She knew Levi would stay to watch over her.

Despite the effects of the drug, Cassie found herself unable to sleep as her mind relentlessly replayed the details of the crash, refusing to grant her any respite. Tears streamed down her face as she realized that JD might not make it.

She was utterly dependent on his presence in her life. To her, they were like two puzzle pieces that perfectly fit together, creating a beautiful and complete picture. With Henry Kyle, they made a family that was ideal in every way—perhaps not the most stable, but undeniably perfect.

Cassie felt an overwhelming sense of desperation for JD to recuperate. At that moment, she thought it was the only viable option. As she finally drifted asleep, her subconscious conjured a vivid dream featuring multiple malevolent individuals tampering with JD's airbag. In her dream, they sneered, "You got what you deserve for putting me in jail."

Chapter Seven

WITH TEARS STREAMING down her cheeks, Cassie leaned in and softly whispered, "I love you," to JD, who lay motionless in a coma. She delicately brushed aside his tousled, golden locks from his furrowed forehead and tenderly smoothed away the forming crease. Her excitement grew with the possibility that he had heard her, potentially explaining his reaction. With urgency, she dashed to the door and called out to the closest medical personnel, her voice filled with hope and concern, "I believe he's starting to wake up!"

Cassie caught the nurse's wide-eyed, startled expression as she witnessed an entire medical team hurriedly entering JD's room, disregarding her presence and urgently pushing her aside.

Feeling hopeful and frightened, Cassie clasped her hands tightly and fervently prayed for JD to wake up, her heart heavy with worry. With her eyes tightly shut, she desperately hoped that her pleas would reach the heavens.

Considering not being religious, she held onto a glimmer of hope that her prayers would be answered.

Despite her desire for him to wake, she was aware that he shouldn't, as the hospital had administered drugs to induce him and was waiting for the swelling in his brain to decrease before allowing him to regain consciousness.

"Miss McKay."

Cassie, with a worried look on her face, turned to the doctor who was on duty in the ICU. "Yes?" She suppressed the bubbling excitement within her and consciously projected an image of poise and self-possession.

"We are dedicatedly focused on reducing the swelling in Mr. Walker's brain. At this point, it is not advisable to awaken him from the medically induced coma."

Her hope dwindled like a flickering candle in a dark room. "But is he waking?"

Shaking his head in concern, the doctor reached out for her elbow with a reassuring touch. He carefully guided her outside the door, ensuring she was safely out of the way as the hospital staff busily emerged from JD's room. "No. It's not uncommon that we see activity while in a coma. He may hear you, and his brain is attempting to react. We're unsure of the extent of this, but we encourage families to speak with their loved ones when they're in this state."

Cassie had no issue with the situation, but she specifically desired to talk with JD while he was fully alert and conscious. "I see." She nervously bit her lip and pondered how best to approach the question. "Will you ever wake him?"

The doctor nodded in agreement, affirming, "Yes. The swelling in his brain has subsided to a level where we can consider waking him. Although there is still some remaining swelling to address, the situation is no longer as precarious."

Cassie took a moment to close her eyes, allowing the sensation of relief to wash over her like a gentle wave, permeating every inch of her being. Soon. "Thank you, Doctor—"

"Wilcox," he finished.

She shook her head slowly and apologetically. "I'm sorry, Doctor Wilcox. Thank you," she said, with a hint of gratitude.

Cassie quietly stepped into JD's brightly lit room, a small smile gently playing on her lips as she tried to conceal the disappointment and concern in her voice.

As she approached him, her heart raced. "So, my love, you wanted some attention, huh? Was it one of the nurses?" she teased with a twinkle in her eye. She adjusted the covers, tucking them around his chest, and murmured, "The doctor is quite handsome, don't you think?"

JD remained impassive, and a wave of despair washed over her, drowning any lingering hope. It seemed she had no choice but to heed the doctor's advice, at least for now.

Levi reentered the room, carefully balancing two steaming cups of freshly brewed coffee in his hands. "Anything new?"

Cassie was on the verge of confiding in him about JD's acknowledgment of her, but she hesitated, fearing that she might come across as foolish. Instead of relaying the scene, she emphatically shook her head. "No," she stated firmly.

"Don't worry, kiddo. It won't be much longer, and he'll be awake."

"Yeah, but he'll still have swelling on his brain. That's dangerous." She grasped JD's hand tightly, ensuring she avoided disturbing the IV needle. As Levi extended a warm cup of coffee to her, she accepted it graciously with her free hand. Thankfully, the lidless coffee cup meant she didn't have to let go of JD's hand until she absolutely had to. She swiftly performed a series of calculations and realized that visiting hours was nearing completion.

Levi raised the cup to his lips, taking a slow, deliberate sip before nodding in acknowledgment. "Yeah, but the doctors will be able to control it."

Cassie's mind was consumed with the need to understand the medical condition causing concern, prompting her to delve into comprehensive research. She felt an urgent obligation to absorb as much knowledge as possible, increasing her sense of determination. If Levi hadn't insisted that she get some sleep last night and this morning, she would have already completed the task.

Levi locked eyes with her, holding her gaze with an intensity that sent a shiver down her spine. "Gus called. They have a case."

Cassie shook her head gently as she firmly stated, "I'm not leaving him."

Levi nodded slowly and offered her a sincere and serious smile. "We expected that, so I promised to help later today. Would you like to come since you can't be here?"

Cassie was torn between wanting to be alone and being with others. She couldn't decide, so she shrugged, showing her uncertainty. After savoring a sip of her rich, fragrant coffee, she gracefully nodded in agreement and said, "I'll come." She also intended to conduct her research at the office to gather information about the truck. Levi's concern had stemmed from the possibility that someone might have interfered with the airbag. While it seemed unlikely, she felt compelled to investigate and find out the truth.

After the accident, law enforcement promptly towed the truck. Cassie made arrangements for it to undergo inspection this morning. Uncertain about the duration of the inspection, she remained hopeful that it would only last a few hours.

"Ladies and gentlemen, please be informed that morning visiting hours in the ICU have concluded. You may return at 1:30 and 5:30 today."

Cassie's heart sank as she let out a heavy sigh. She found it difficult to part ways with JD in such a manner, but she understood that it was necessary. As she gently released his hand, she leaned in close and kissed his cheek tenderly. "Get well soon, JD," she whispered.

She stood straight and brought the warm Styrofoam cup of coffee to her lips, taking in the comforting aroma before indulging in a sip. Her day ahead seemed demanding despite having enjoyed a decent night's sleep. She knew she'd need plenty of coffee to keep her energized. Despite her reluctance to acknowledge it, Cassie still felt deeply fatigued from her injuries' aftermath. She realized she needed a significant rest period—that elusive measurement of time known as a "fortnight" escaped her understanding.

"Let's go, kiddo." Levi guided her gracefully out of the room, down the elevator, and towards his sleek, rented SUV, waiting to whisk them away.

Cassie was unable to lift her spirits despite the medical staff's assurances that they didn't expect JD to die. She couldn't believe in their assurances until they woke him, and he spoke to her.

"How about a doughnut?"

To boost her morale, she agreed with Levi's suggestion, "Why not?" even though she had no appetite.

With a warm smile, Levi courteously opened the SUV door for her, carefully handed her the seatbelt, and swiftly made his way to the driver's seat. As he started the vehicle, he turned to her with a curious expression and inquired, "What happened while I was gone?"

Her attempt to deceive him had clearly failed. "I thought JD was waking," she murmured, her words barely audible as tears overflowed from her eyes. Hiding her face in her hands, she made no effort to stem the tears, feeling no shame in displaying her vulnerability in front of Levi. "I thought he'd heard me."

"Oh, kiddo." Levi leaned in and gently massaged her shoulder, applying a comforting and soothing touch. "He'll be awake soon enough, then you two can be married."

The situation made her cry even harder. JD wouldn't want to get married immediately, especially with a broken arm. He always emphasized that he wanted her special day to be perfect. Although he was unaware, the concept of "perfect" encompassed the unity of the three of them—JD, Henry Kyle, and her—being together.

"Let's find something for you to work on. It might help take your mind off things for a while."

Tears welled up in her eyes, and she could only nod. "Okay," she whispered, her voice choked with emotion. Despite her reluctance, she agreed to do some work to show gratitude to Levi for his kindness.

"Your mother called to say she'll be home this afternoon. Will you be okay with picking her up?"

Once again, her mother's flight was canceled because of the weather, leaving her frustrated and desiring her mother's empathy, much like a child seeking comfort and understanding.

With her hands slowly lowering, she sniffed once more and then stated confidently, "I can pick her up."

Levi handed her a tissue, a small gesture of comfort amidst the emotional exchange. As he skillfully maneuvered the SUV in reverse, the parking space was soon behind them, and they smoothly exited the parking lot.

Cassie gently dabbed her teary eyes with a tissue before blowing her nose.

During their ride, they rode past a quaint doughnut shop. Levi ordered her a delightful Bavarian Crème chocolate-covered doughnut. She hungrily devoured the treat, not realizing how hungry she was. After all, who could resist the temptation of a warm, delicious doughnut?

As they rolled onto the seashell-studded parking lot of Coastal Investigation, Cassie carefully resumed her cheerful facade. She was adamant about not wanting sympathy from anyone, nor did she seek any extra attention. All she desired at that moment was simply to exist.

As Levi and Cassie entered the office, Daisy, the assistant, met them. Daisy welcomed Levi with a warm

"Hi" before turning her attention to Cassie. "Hey there, I just wanted to let you know that the police department tried to reach you. The chief mentioned that he had called your cell several times already."

Finally, the much-awaited answers. However, as Cassie pondered, she wondered whether she genuinely desired them. She was conflicted. She didn't want to know, but she felt a compelling need to find out. The burning question remained: had someone deliberately caused harm to JD?

Levi graciously pulled out a chair for her at her desk, and in response, she beamed at him with appreciation. "Thanks."

With a nod, he settled into his chair at the desk and lifted the lid of his laptop, ready to begin his work.

Cassie carefully lifted the pink slip, reading the message before anxiously dialing the number.

Chapter Eight

HENRY KYLE STRAINED every muscle in his body as he and his fellow campers worked together to navigate the boat according to the instructions of the camp counselors. Despite his exhausted arms, he persisted, recalling his father's instructions from their sailing expeditions. Approaching the roaring rapids, a surge of excitement overcame him. The adrenaline-inducing nature of outdoor sports made him ponder what he had missed out on in traditional schooling. He wondered if the group participated in ziplining and rafting or played only football and baseball. To find out, he planned to ask his new friend, Noah.

Noah made his home in Ocean Springs, the next coastal town from Gulf Islands, where he attended the local middle school. Despite frequently vocalizing his disdain for school, Noah often reminisced about the positive aspects, such as his supportive teachers, close friends, and engaging in extracurricular activities. He appeared to dislike the schoolwork and his English teacher strongly. Nonetheless, Henry Kyle didn't have any problem with either of them.

The boat sliced through the water, sending sparkling droplets flying as it navigated around the first imposing rock. The river didn't present a formidable rapid; however, its exhilaration to the group was undeniable. He wondered if his dad and Miss Cassie would be up for hitting bigger rapids this summer.

Henry Kyle felt a growing sense of worry about his father's health. Every night, he diligently dialed the phone, but Miss Cassie always picked up, providing updates on his father's activities, whether he was sleeping or working. Despite exchanging brief words with her, it never felt quite right for Henry Kyle. All he longed for was to engage in a meaningful conversation with his dad.

Mrs. Davis leaned closer toward him, indicating her desire to be heard over the rushing water. "Dig in deep, Henry Kyle!"

Despite her age, the woman exuded an abundance of energy. He found himself drawn to her, and the feeling seemed mutual. She has shown kindness to both Noah and him throughout the past few days.

Had it truly only been a few days? It felt like an eternity had passed since this all began. They had been eagerly engaged in many activities, including lively games, creating intricate crafts—even though he found that activity less appealing—and enjoying each other's company while sharing captivating stories. Despite their enjoyment, they were apprehensive about the rapid passing of the two weeks.

Shouting to be heard over the roaring water, he exclaimed, "I've got it!" Despite the searing pain in his arms, he remained resolute in his determination not to let her down.

"Kids," she announced loudly, "pull in your oars!"

As they approached the ride's conclusion, Henry Kyle felt relief wash over him. Nevertheless, he was utterly drained and knew he required a respite before embarking on the same journey later in the week.

After safely landing on firm ground, he grabbed a towel to dry himself and laughed with Noah.

Mrs. Davis strode up to them with a warm smile. "I hope the ride was enjoyable for you?" she asked kindly.

Henry Kyle and his companion both vigorously nodded their heads in agreement. "Yes, ma'am," Henry Kyle affirmed.

"Such a well-mannered young man," she replied warmly.

Henry Kyle hesitated as Mrs. Davis prepared to leave. "Mrs. Davis," he said, a note of concern in his voice, "I know our regular phone time is tonight, but could I call my dad now? I'm worried he might be sick."

Her smile slowly turned into a pensive expression, and he found comfort in the fact that she cared enough to be worried about him. The camp leadership showed wisdom in entrusting her to manage the counselors, but most teenagers needed more confidence regarding their duties. "Sure. Come to my office after you change clothes."

Henry Kyle dashed through the winding paths of the forest, his footsteps kicking up leaves as he made his way to his shared cabin. With haste, he changed into a fresh set of clothes and then raced through the bustling hub of the camp to reach Mrs. Davis's office. Upon arrival, he awaited her presence as she discussed with various counselors.

Henry Kyle sighed deeply as he pondered whether his dad and Miss Cassie would permit him to attend the camp again the following year.

When the counselors exited Mrs. Davis's office, she called him in.

"Thank you, Mrs. Davis."

"Anything for you, child."

Henry Kyle gingerly picked up the shiny, black desk phone and dialed his dad's cell. If only he had been permitted to bring a cell phone to camp, he could have easily dialed his dad's number at any time of the day or night, allowing them to catch up with each other. After two rings, Miss Cassie answered.

"Hello?"

He exuded an air of sadness as he stood there. Miss Cassie kept answering his dad's phone, indicating his father was unwell. Since arriving at camp, he had been unable to converse with his dad. This was unusual, as even when his dad was on assignment, he always made time for him.

"Hi, Miss Cassie. I wanted to speak with my dad."

"Oh, honey, he's in an interview and will be tied up for hours. I can let him know you called. Was there a reason for the call?"

Was Miss Cassie telling him the truth? Was his dad genuinely occupied with work and unable to speak with him? "No reason. I was just worried about him."

"Oh, Henry Kyle, don't worry about your dad. He's waiting for you to come home. We both are."

He knew he should head home—perhaps his dad needed him—but the anticipation of their visit to the zoo the next day was exciting. He was especially eager to see the baby alligators.

"What did you do today?" she asked.

His eyes sparkled with excitement as he recounted the exhilarating experience. "We had an amazing time rafting. Although it wasn't white water rafting, it was still an incredible adventure. Can we tackle some real big waves when I come home?"

Miss Cassie's laughter filtered over the phone, bringing a smile to his face as he reveled in the joyful sound. "I'm sure we can. I think your dad would love that."

Without much thought, he blurted out, "Can I return next year?"

"I don't see why not. Do you like it there?"

"Yes, ma'am."

"Okay, I'll get your dad to agree. Is that a pact?"

With a broad smile on his face, Henry Kyle exclaimed in a triumphant tone, "Yes!"

"Okay, I will let you get back to the fun."

"Will you tell Dad I called?"

"I sure will. Bye. Love you." She ended the call.

Henry Kyle gently lifted the phone away from his ear and placed it back into the cradle, thoughtfully expressing, "Miss Cassie says my dad is just working, so he can't talk to me."

Mrs. Davis raised an eyebrow. "Oh?"

Henry Kyle sat down in the chair, his legs swinging back and forth uneasily as he grimaced, lost in thought. "Yeah, I think he's really sick or hurt, and I'm worried."

"What makes you worried?"

"Well, he promised to talk with me every night. I haven't spoken to him at all." The persistent concern continued to invade his thoughts, making it impossible for him to fend off the looming shadows.

"I tell you what," Mrs. Davis said. "If you're still worried in a few days, I'll take you home to see your dad. How does that sound?"

Henry Kyle jumped up in excitement, exclaiming, "That would be awesome!"

She laughed. "Okay, it'll be our secret. Now, get back to the rest of the kids. I believe you're making shell picture frames this afternoon."

Henry Kyle's expression turned sour. "More crafts," he said with disappointment.

"Perk up. I think that Miss Cassie you spoke with might like one."

"Do you really think so?" he asked with excitement shining in his eyes. It hadn't occurred to him to create something for Miss Cassie, who held a special place in his dad's heart. "Okay."

He felt lucky to have Mrs. Davis with him as he hurried away. He requested that she bring him home ahead of schedule if he could not communicate with his dad in the coming days. He felt the strong need to be present to provide support in case his father was unwell or injured.

After that conversation, he sat down next to Noah.

"Did you get your dad?" Noah's expression twisted in frustration as he struggled to affix a delicate seashell to the edge of the frame.

"No, but Mrs. Davis said she'd bring me home early if I can't reach him soon."

Noah looked up with concern etched on his face. "I don't think she can do that. My dad said we're not to get into a vehicle with counselors unless it's all of us and a camp van."

Henry Kyle shook that off. "It's my dad we're talking about. Of course, I'll allow her to take me to him."

Chapter Nine

BEFORE CASSIE COULD call the police chief's number, her phone suddenly rang, interrupting her. With impatience evident in her voice and full attention fixed on the airbag, she grunted out a curt, "Hello."

"Miss McKay, this is Police Chief Grant of the Gulfport Police Department."

The phone call from the police chief of the town where the accident occurred didn't offer hope for a positive answer to the pressing question about the airbag.

"Hello, Chief Grant."

His heavy sigh carried over the phone. Cassie closed her eyes, fearing the following words to come out of this man's mouth.

"I guess you know why I'm calling."

"I do." *Just get on with it already.*

"We've completed our interviews with the witnesses to the accident."

Cassie couldn't care less about that.

"We still haven't located the driver who hit Mr. Walker's truck. But we did complete the inspection of his vehicle."

"And?" Her heart thudded in her chest, refusing to entertain the idea that anyone would deliberately cause harm to the man she cherished.

"The vehicle checked out fine."

Cassie felt a wave of relief washing over her. She realized that it was just a malfunction. Her JD was now in the hospital, while the other driver was still out there, roaming free.

"Thank you, Chief—"

"But there's one thing," he said gently, interrupting her.

Cassie felt a knot tightening in her stomach as the Chief continued speaking, rendering her unable to utter a single word.

"Our inspection revealed that the driver-side airbag, which did not deploy in the accident, had been tampered with before the incident."

The situation had turned into her worst nightmare. The airbag meant to protect JD had been deliberately disabled, and they were forced off the road by the same person or a bizarre twist of fate. Was she seeking one or two culprits?

"Do you," she hesitated before clearing her throat, "know who disabled it?"

"Not at this time. We think the accident and the airbag might be tied together. No clues lead us that way except the coincidence, but that's our working theory."

"Will you update me on finding the vehicle that ran us off the road?"

"Sure thing, Miss McKay." The police chief ended the call before Cassie could ask another question. She knew she owed the man more than that but couldn't handle a detailed discussion about what had happened.

Cassie remained composed as she carefully set her phone on the desk, her gaze fixed on the horizon. She couldn't shake the chilling thought: had someone made an attempt on JD's life? The only lead the police department had was the unsettling coincidence.

Levi, Gus, Nan, and Daisy suddenly loomed over her, their anxious expressions revealing their anticipation of the chief's response regarding the accident.

Cassie's eyes welled up with tears as she gazed at Levi with a mixture of sadness and frustration, and then she uttered, "It was sabotage."

Chapter Ten

ONCE SHE ARRIVED home, Cassie fell into her mother's comforting embrace. After remaining stoic all day, the floodgates opened, and tears poured out.

"Honey, I'm so sorry I wasn't here for you." Patricia's arms tightened around her. "Now, now." She rubbed her hands lightly up and down Cassie's back, soothing her.

Cassie hesitantly pulled away, her tear-streaked face breaking into a soft laugh as she glanced at her mom. "I'm sorry," she said graciously, reaching for the tissue that Levi kindly handed her.

Twice that day, Levi came to her aid, showing his support and assistance. She eagerly anticipated his regular presence at CI, longing for the days when they used to work side by side as colleagues. Then, it occurred to her that he had stayed at her home long after her mother had returned. She inwardly smiled at that. Perhaps there was a spark between them.

"Thanks, Levi." Cassie gently wiped the tears from her face, sniffled, and then carefully discarded the used tissue into the garbage can in the clean kitchen. She then opened the refrigerator door and plucked a cold, refreshing raspberry sparkling water from the shelf, her favorite choice for a pick-me-up. "Anyone else want anything to drink?"

"I'm good," echoed the two.

Cassie eagerly popped the top of the can, taking a long, refreshing gulp of the cool liquid, feeling it quench her parched throat. Here she was, once again delaying the inevitable. *All right, grab your big girl panties and get this over with.*

As she entered the spacious living room, Cassie's steps faltered. Her mother and Levi were perched closely on the plush couch, their heads bent in whispered conversation. Cassie couldn't help but wonder if their hushed discussion was about her or if they were covertly sharing their feelings for each other.

As they noticed her, the two quickly parted ways, looking as guilty as if they had been caught kissing under the gym bleachers. Patricia sprang to her feet and gestured for Cassie to take her place before sinking into a comfortable, flowery armchair.

Cassie, hoping to buy some time, turned towards Levi with a concerned expression and inquired, "Levi, how are Phoebe and Cooper doing?"

"They're fine." He pointed to a knit in his jeans. "Phoebe welcomed me with a climb up my leg."

Cassie couldn't help but smile at the sight. The kitten had a notorious habit of swiftly climbing up on things, too impatient to wait for someone to pick her up. "And Cooper?"

Levi's brow furrowed as he recounted the situation. "He watched me from the doorway and then ran off when I approached him."

Cooper remained frightened of unfamiliar faces. While he showed great affection toward Henry Kyle, JD, and her, the presence of others instilled a deep-seated fear in him. Cassie couldn't help but wonder about the unspeakable torment he might have experienced before being deposited at the shelter.

When she realized Levi had nothing more to say, she turned to her mom. "How was the trip?"

Patricia lifted her brows as if to say, "So, that's how we're playing it." Cassie knew those looks well and could decipher every single one.

"Well, it was fun. That was until Judy fell and broke her hip. That drained most of the excitement from the trip. But we still enjoyed ourselves and plan to do this once a year." She laughed lightly. "Without the broken hip, of course."

Her mother had a knack for condensing a couple of weeks into just a few sentences, especially when eagerly anticipating news from her daughter.

"More, please."

Her mother huffed, then smiled at her daughter. "The cruise was amazing. Too much food, though." She patted her flat belly. "I think I gained ten pounds. But we enjoyed it. You can't believe everything you can do on one of those big boats. It was worth the expense."

"That's good. How is Judy now?"

"She's fine. Her kids were at the airport, ready to take care of her. Now, you don't have to tell me everything, but tell me you're okay and update me on JD's condition."

Bless her mom. She always shared everything with her because they had such a close relationship, but the fact that her mom didn't ask about her well-being until she was ready to discuss it made her heart swell with love. "I'm doing okay. Just a few bruises from the seat belt and this little scratch." She gestured to the small wound on the side of her head from broken glass. It wasn't big, but she wanted to ensure her mother noticed it first. "My shoulder and arm are sore where I rolled on them, but it doesn't hamper any motion."

"Let me see." Patricia stood up from her seat and walked over to Cassie. With a concerned look on her face, she carefully inspected the stitched cut on Cassie's head, making sure to assess the severity of the injury. "Could have been worse." She returned to her seat.

Cassie's words poured forth, detailing every event since her mother's departure on vacation, culminating in the journey and JD's hospitalization.

During her recitation, Patricia remained silent, her eyes fixed on her daughter. Her friend Levi offered occasional reassurance by gently patting Cassie's shoulder. Levi's supportive presence and encouragement meant a great deal to her. As she completed her recitation, her mother nervously bit her lip. Cassie pondered whether she had picked up that habit from her mother or vice versa. Regardless, it was a distinct family trait, revealing their shared approach to processing thoughts.

"That's a lot for a mother to take in. I'm glad you're okay, and Henry Kyle wasn't in the truck. Can we see JD?"

"He's still in ICU, and they limit the number of visitors to two, but I imagine we can get you in there with me when Levi isn't." As she turned to Levi, a warm smile lit up her face. "Did he mention that he told them he was my father?"

Patricia's eyebrows rose again, and Cassie took them as the "what did you say?" gesture. "He did now?"

Levi fidgeted in his seat, then absently played with a crease in his jeans. "Well, I knew she needed someone with her until you returned, and it seemed the only way." His smile toward Patricia revealed an unspoken depth to their relationship, sending a surge of excitement through Cassie. She was bursting with the urge to share the news with JD.

JD. She felt immense sorrow for him as he lay in a coma for what seemed like an eternity. If only he didn't have to be in the hospital at all, she thought as she anxiously waited by his side. As she mulled over her plans, she glanced at her watch. Only one more hour remained before visiting time. She decided to bring her mom along this time. Having Levi by her side was terrific, but nothing could compare to the comforting presence of her mother. The support and love of a parent meant more to her than anything else.

"I'm leaving in about half an hour if you want to go with me, Mom."

"That's my cue to leave." Levi stood.

"No, you're welcome to stay until we leave." Cassie patted the seat he'd vacated.

Levi smiled softly down at her. "I believe I have a case to investigate."

That's right. Gus and Nan would need Levi. "How long can you stay?" How long would they need him?

"As long as needed. I submitted my retirement papers before I hopped on the plane to see you. I'll need to return and pack up my place soon, but I'm here to stay."

Cassie leaped up and embraced him in a tight hug. "That's the most wonderful news I've heard all day," she exclaimed with a glowing smile.

"So, my amazing vacation meant nothing?" Patricia teased.

Stepping back from Levi, Cassie's laughter rang out. She treasured the presence of these two. They had been her unwavering support through the tumultuous times she had faced, and she knew she could rely on them to help navigate the challenges that awaited her.

She reminded herself of the deliberate act of sabotage. Someone had tampered with JD's airbag, intending to cause him harm. She was sure JD would recover, and they would stop at nothing to uncover the perpetrator, no matter their challenges.

Chapter Eleven

UPON CAREFUL CONSIDERATION, I find myself with no alternative. Additionally, another attorney has advised me that I lack sufficient grounds to pursue custody. The entire fate hinged on JD Walker's willingness to undergo a DNA test. However, she doubted he would, fearing that taking the test might lead to the heartbreaking prospect of losing Henry Kyle, a child whom he had always believed to be his own.

The doctors may soon wake JD from his medically induced coma. I can't wait any longer to ensure he is out of my way. I have found someone working at the hospital to blackmail, but I doubt their ability to follow through even though I could ruin them. Once they have completed my assigned task, Henry Kyle must be relocated hastily before someone discovers him and takes him to his fake dad's funeral. His kidnapper-dad's funeral. He kept Henry Kyle, knowing the woman had been unfaithful to him.

"Mrs. Davis."

I am starting to dislike that name and the teenage volunteers. They are unable to do anything by themselves. This generation has been affected by several significant shifts in parenting and technology. The approach of using time-outs instead of physical punishment and grounding and the prevalence of excessive screen time through TV and video games has changed how children interact with their environment. This shift has reduced the time kids spend playing and socializing outdoors with their peers in the neighborhood, potentially impacting their development and social skills.

We raised their parents with a strong emphasis on adhering to rules and facing consequences rather than receiving participation trophies. We now find ourselves questioning where we may have made missteps.

"Yes, Kerry." My voice trembles with frustration, and I watch as the girl flinches in response. Knowing she's been a constant irritant since the beginning is satisfying. She applied for the leadership position among volunteers but was displeased when she did not get chosen, and I did.

"Henry Kyle wants to speak with you. He's still worried about his father."

Of course, he was. I wonder what explanation that woman provided regarding JD's unavailability. I highly doubt she was forthright. The young boy displayed remarkable intelligence, perhaps bordering on being too intelligent for his age. We'll see.

"Send him to me."

"Okay."

What has become of "Yes, ma'am?" These children were simply intolerable. No one has taken the time to instill them with proper manners. Once again, my generation has raised their children with care and guidance, only to receive disrespect in return.

"Oh, and Kerry?"

With her hand on the doorknob, the volunteer turned. "Yes?"

"After you tell Henry Kyle, look at the inventory of the rafting supplies. I think we lost a paddle out there."

"No, they were–"

If only I had the time, I would ensure that she faces consequences for her impertinence. Unfortunately, time is not on my side. I need to find a way to separate her from the situation. Compared to the other campers, she's too interested in my relationship with Henry Kyle.

"Just double-check."

Kerry shrugs. "Okay." She turns and closes the door behind her.

As I sat at my desk, a surge of frustration coursed through me, compelling me to want to hurl something at it. However, I knew I had to keep my emotions in check. I made a silent promise to myself that I would do everything in my power to ensure that Henry Kyle didn't grow up with that same kind of destructive anger. My vision for him was that of a respectful young man who embodied Southern etiquette principles, always defending his elders.

I imagined him as someone who conducted himself with impeccable manners, steered clear of trouble, and excelled academically, ultimately becoming a shining star at an esteemed private school. It angers me that JD has permitted my grandson to be homeschooled by someone who isn't even a real teacher. I will correct that mistake immediately.

The sudden rap on my door jolts me out of my reverie about the future I envision with my grandson. "Enter."

Henry Kyle entered the room with a troubled look on his face. "Mrs. Davis," he said as he took a seat, "I haven't been able to get in touch with my dad yet."

Leaning forward, I rest my forearms on the desk, interlacing my fingers to prevent accidental contact, even with Henry Kyle. "It's perfect timing because I just got a call. I'm sorry to say it, but your dad is in the hospital."

The young boy looked utterly shattered, with his eyes filled with sadness and confusion. Every fiber of my being longed to reach out and envelop him in a warm embrace until his little heart found solace. Meanwhile, Henry Kyle shifted to the edge of his seat, engrossed in the unfolding situation. "What's wrong with him? How long has he been sick? Can I call someone to pick me up and take me to him?"

I extended my hand gently, signaling to halt further inquiries and allowing the young child to catch his breath. He shows care and concern for his captor, which deeply upsets me. I don't want him to grieve for the man once he's no longer with us. Henry Kyle's affection should be solely for me, as I am the only family he has left in the world.

"I'm not certain what's wrong with him or how long he's been there, but your father's fiancée wanted me to tell you the truth." I can't believe her name slipped my mind. Hopefully, Henry Kyle wouldn't notice.

"Miss Cassie?"

"Yes, Miss Cassie."

A glistening teardrop slowly trickled down his cheek, and an intense urge to gently brush it away surged through me. However, I restrained myself. Not yet. "Why wouldn't she tell me instead of giving me excuses why Dad couldn't talk to me?"

The anguish etched on the boy's face pierces my heart like a sharp stake. I ponder whether I should have fabricated a comforting falsehood to assuage his distress. Nonetheless, I am determined to rectify the situation and bring him solace.

Chapter Twelve

ENTERING JD'S ICU room, Patricia enveloped Cassie in a supportive embrace, her voice filled with compassion and sorrow as she took in the sight of JD's frail state. He generally radiated strength and confidence, but it would have pained him to know that his vulnerable moments were displayed for others to witness.

Cassie melted into her mother's embrace, drawing on the unspoken support and solace that came with the comforting touch. She silently motioned for Patricia to take the solitary chair in the sparsely furnished room.

"No, honey, you sit." Her mother's tone was unwavering, yet her eyes conveyed a sense of urgency. She silently pleaded with Cassie to grasp the gravity of the situation.

"It's okay, Mom. I'll sit on the edge of the bed." Her desperate need to touch JD stemmed from the sight of him lying in bed, appearing as though he was on the verge of death. She longed to feel his presence and vitality.

Patricia glanced at the bed and nodded. "Well, okay, then."

Cassie sat gently on the edge of the hospital bed, intertwining her fingers with JD's hand, which lay free from the tangle of IV lines. "JD, honey, I'm back. Look who I brought with me." She gazed at her mother, tilting her head in JD's direction.

"Oh." Patricia's voice trembled as she nervously cleared her throat. "Hi, JD," she greeted, her shoulders lifting slightly as she gestured with her hands, silently asking, "Is that enough?"

She felt an urge to chuckle at her mother's visible uncertainty. All her life, her mother had been her pillar of strength. Without a word, she nodded in response to her mother's silent query, providing all the assurance needed.

She turned back to JD, struggling to hold back her tears. She was determined not to cry in front of him. He needed her to stay strong and composed, not just for him but also for Henry Kyle.

Thoughts of Henry Kyle stirred up a familiar ache in her heart. She couldn't shake the guilt of lying to the boy repeatedly. Would Henry Kyle ever find it in his heart to forgive her for concealing his father's hospitalization? She thought it over and realized it would take quite some time, but she knew it would be an obstacle she needed to overcome before she and JD could get married.

When she and JD had the accident, they hadn't specified a particular day, only two weeks. "JD, you must fight this. Please be here to assist me in planning our wedding. I don't want to handle everything on my own."

Patricia leaned forward in the creaky armchair. Her eyes filled with anticipation. "Wedding? Have you set the date?" she asked eagerly.

Despite the solemn atmosphere, a smile unconsciously graced her lips. "Yes, we'd discussed two weeks, but now...." Her voice faltered at the last word, and the smile faded from her face.

The door swung open, and a calm and friendly nurse stepped inside, greeting the room with a warm smile. "Hello," he announced softly, lifting a syringe in one hand. "I'm here to provide Mr. Walker with his medication."

Cassie was face to face with a tall man she didn't recognize. Grasping the situation, she knew that the ICU was severely short-staffed and often had to pull nurses from other floors. "Let me move," she insisted, determined to navigate the challenging circumstances.

He shook his head. "No, you're fine where you are."

As JD lay in the hospital bed, the nurse carefully inserted the needle into his IV drip, slowly plunging the syringe's contents into the line. His eyes darted back and forth between the syringe and the bag of liquid hanging from the IV pole, ensuring a precise and steady delivery of the medication into JD's system.

Cassie hesitated, wanting to inquire about the treatment being administered, but she assumed she wouldn't comprehend the explanation anyway. Ultimately, she trusted the staff, believing they would make the best decisions for JD.

After meticulously tending to the patient, the nurse turned to Cassie and flashed a warm, reassuring smile. "That should help him sleep soundly," he said. With a sense of urgency, the nurse hurried out of the room, likely dashing off to assist another patient. Cassie couldn't help but feel empathy for the staff here. Despite their exceptional skills, the persistent issue of being short-staffed had taken its toll, leaving them visibly fatigued from working additional shifts.

Cassie was horrified at the idea of another drug being administered to JD. She desperately wanted to shout, "I don't want him to sleep. I want him to wake up!" However, she restrained herself because of the hospital setting. This internal outburst did little to ease her distress, so she voiced it to her mother.

Patricia rose from her seat and hugged her daughter. "We all do." Straightening, she said, "Sweetheart, I'm going to go and see if I can rustle us up some coffee."

Cassie maintained unyielding eye contact with JD as she nodded her agreement, displaying complete disregard for refreshments while her fiancé slept.

Cassie engaged in her usual routine in solitude—talking to JD and fretting with his covers. She paid no mind to whether he could hear her or not. The lingering hope that he could listen prompted her to continue speaking. "Well, I've lied to Henry Kyle again." Her eyes filled with regret as she spoke, "You know he's never going to forgive me for this," she said with a heavy heart, shaking her head. "Not that I blame him."

As a soon-to-be parent, she now understood the heavy burden of making tough decisions for the well-being of one's children. She realized that instead of being by his father's hospital bedside, Henry Kyle deserved to be at camp, enjoying and having a fulfilling time.

"Will it always be this hard? To make decisions for Henry Kyle's sake that we know he won't like?" She heaved a weary sigh. "Maybe I'm not cut out to be a parent because it's ripping my heart to shreds, knowing he may hate me for this."

"Honey—"

Cassie's peaceful reverie with JD was shattered by the abrupt interruption of her mother's words, pulling her back to reality.

"—you'll always have this problem." Patricia handed her a steaming coffee cup filled with the aroma of freshly brewed coffee. "But you need to do it. You must have the fortitude to guide the youth until they understand the consequences of their actions and decisions."

As the scalding coffee rushed over Cassie's tongue, it startled her senses, triggering a temporary diversion from her jumbled emotions. There was a fierce internal struggle within her—part of her wished for an intimate conversation solely between her and JD, while the other part cherished her mother's perspective. It was undoubtedly a perplexing situation.

Her hand clasped tightly around JD's hand, and she turned to her mother with a furrowed brow. "Will it always be this tough and challenging?" she asked, her voice filled with uncertainty.

Patricia mustered a feeble smile and nodded in agreement. "It'll get tougher once he becomes a teenager and feels he can make decisions without you."

The image of a teenage Henry Kyle suddenly appeared in Cassie's mind, and a smile graced her lips. However, her smile wavered as she imagined his future appearance, resembling nothing of his father. A sudden realization washed over her, causing the coffee in her stomach to sour. Was JD Henry Kyle's father? What if he wasn't? Would they lose him?

"But don't worry," Patricia continued, oblivious of Cassie's despair, "they'll come around in the end. You did."

She always observed that her mother never displayed strictness towards her; only her stepfathers did. She often speculated that this differential treatment was because she wasn't their biological child. *Oh, wow. Am I subconsciously imitating the behavior of one of my stepfathers toward me? Am I being sterner because he's not my biological son?* She couldn't shake off these thoughts, even though she found it hard to believe them. Nonetheless, the uncertainty troubled her deeply.

To conceal her concern from her mother, she mustered a smile. "I did, didn't I?"

"Well, you weren't the worst child. You were actually pretty good."

She lived in constant fear of a potential spanking, an experience that she was sure her mother would never subject her to but one that she believed one of her stepfathers would administer without hesitation. The mere thought of him sent shivers down her spine. After her mother had divorced the man who had tried to, she abruptly cut off that thought, realizing that now was not the time to dwell on it.

"Am I wrong lying to Henry Kyle and keeping him at summer camp?"

In Cassie's mind, her mother's response seemed to take an eternity, but she was grateful for her thoughtful consideration instead of a hasty reply.

"It's what I would have done with you. There's nothing he can do. He can't even visit his father, can he?"

Cassie pondered the minimum age requirement but dismissed its significance, assuming that the hospital would likely make an exception. With a nonchalant shrug, she brushed off the concern. "I'm not sure."

"No matter." Patricia shook her head. "Henry Kyle has been looking forward to his first summer camp all year. It's all he's asked about when I've been schooling him. It would be a pity to take that away from him when all he could do was sit around and worry."

True. But— And that word kept creeping up too often. But, what if JD didn't— She swallowed the lump grappled around her throat. —Didn't make it?

Cassie squeezed her eyes shut, trying to block out the overwhelming emotional pain that threatened to engulf her. She knew she couldn't allow herself to dwell on these thoughts. This was supposed to be treatable…at least, that's what the doctors had promised her.

The thought of doctors triggered the appearance of one: the on-call doctor, Dr. Miles. He entered the room with a comforting smile and greeted, "Hello, Ms. McKay. The swelling on Mr. Walker's brain has decreased significantly, and we're now at a point where we can proceed to wake him."

As Cassie gently slid from the edge of the bed, anticipation filled her heart at the thought of what was to come. "But the nurse just administered something to help him sleep. Does that mean we have to wait?" She couldn't bear the idea of waiting longer. Determined, she planned to make strong coffee, fetch an energy drink for JD, and do whatever was necessary to keep him awake once they roused him.

Perplexed, the physician inquired, "Did you say sleep?" while reviewing the patient's chart. "I didn't prescribe any medications this morning and don't observe any records of administered substances."

Cassie attempted to voice a protest, but her words were cut short as JD's vital signs suddenly plummeted, and his heart ceased to beat.

Chapter Thirteen

AS JD SLOWLY regained consciousness, he was surrounded by the steady beeping of medical equipment. His heavy eyes struggled to open, and his head throbbed with a strange sensation. The sharp ache in his arm demanded his attention, and as he focused his vision, he made out the figures of people in lab coats and scrubs, their faces obscured by blurriness and bright light.

"Ah, you're finally awake," a voice murmured, breaking JD's silence. He struggled to orient himself as his senses slowly returned. Assuming it to be the doctor in the lab coat, JD gradually regained awareness.

JD's parched throat felt scratchy and in desperate need of hydration. He attempted to speak, but only a hoarse, barely audible "water" escaped his lips.

"I bet you'd like some water," the doctor said. "Here."

JD felt a slender straw touching his lips. He eagerly sipped the cool water, relishing every drop, before the cup was gently lifted away from him. Confused, he began to ask, "What—"

"I'm Dr. Myers, and you were in a car accident."

His throat felt tight with fear as he couldn't shake the memory of the accident he had experienced with Cassie. "Cassie?"

"I'm right here," she said softly as she stepped into his line of sight, and a wave of relief washed over him, reaching into the depths of his being.

JD's vision slowly cleared, and as he looked around the room, he noticed the various machines connected to him with their blinking lights and low hum. "What happened?" he managed to utter, his mind still foggy. Vague memories of being struck, the disorienting sensation of spinning, and then the jolting impact of rolling through the air flickered in his mind.

Before Cassie could begin detailing the events of the accident, the doctor carefully lifted one of his eyelids, using a small flashlight to examine it. Then, with equal care, the doctor repeated the process with the other eyelid.

"You have a broken arm and an occurrence of swelling on the brain," Dr. Myers said.

JD's heart raced with alarm, not due to the broken arm but the thought of the swelling. Wasn't that a potentially life-threatening situation? Before JD could voice his concern, the doctor pressed on with his explanation.

"We had you in a medically induced coma while most of the swelling subsided. You still have some minor swelling, but we don't consider it life-threatening."

"How long was I unconscious?" He inquired with a mix of relief and lingering worry.

"It has been nearly a week since your accident. While we have roused you, you must remain in the hospital for several more days to monitor you."

Reluctant to set foot in hospitals, he was acutely aware of the stakes and thus resolved to comply with the doctor's instructions. "That's fine," he murmured, bracing himself for what lay ahead.

The doctor carefully reviewed the medications and treatments that had been administered. However, his attention was squarely fixed on Cassie. Relieved, he noted her seemingly unscathed appearance—minus cuts and bruises—following the accident and silently expressed gratitude.

After the doctor and the nurse left, JD finally found himself alone with Cassie. He took a deep breath, feeling the day's weight lift off his shoulders. With a genuine concern in his voice, he asked her, "How are you feeling?"

She rushed to his bedside and took a seat next to him. "I had a few bruises, but I was mostly fine. My airbags worked, but one of yours didn't."

He felt angry and frustrated, vowing to take legal action against the company for negligence. "I'm so relieved that you're alright," JD said, his hand trembling as he moved it from his uninjured arm—where the IV needle was inserted—and gently caressed her cheek. At that moment, he realized the depth of his love for her, and the thought of her being hurt like him was unbearable.

Her eyes were filled with tears, shining with emotion. "I thought you'd be terrified when the doctor told you that you had flatlined earlier."

JD was taken aback and exclaimed, "What? Did I miss something?" He'd been so focused on Cassie and her well-being that he hadn't heard that he'd coded on the table.

She shyly muttered, "Oh, you missed that part, didn't you?"

Angrily, he grumbled, "Obviously." Then he paused, attempting to ask, "How long was I— How long was I dead?"

Her sudden reaction was evident as she jumped, exclaiming, "Oh, only for a moment. They shocked you right back to life. But it was the longest moment of my life. You were lucky the doctor was here when it happened."

He'd bet. He had died. He realized that he hadn't seen any white lights. This absence left him pondering the implications for his eternal soul.

Levi entered the room with purposeful strides, his confident demeanor filling the space. As he approached JD, he offered a greeting infused with a hint of teasing, "Hello, lazy."

JD attempted to chuckle, but it became a deep, husky rumble. "Yeah, I picked that up from you," he teased in response. He would grapple with his mortality at a later point in time. For now, it was evident that he was very much alive.

Levi paused as he positioned himself on the opposite side of the bed, facing Cassie. "Have you informed him yet?"

Cassie shook her head, and her brow furrowed. Observing her reaction, JD couldn't help but wonder what had transpired.

"Not yet. The doctor just finished with him."

"Tell me what?" he rasped. Good grief, he needed more water. He gestured to it, and Cassie grabbed the glass and brought the straw to his lips. JD never thought water could taste so good.

After JD finished his drink, Cassie gently took the glass away. His sore throat began feeling better, so he asked, "Tell me what?"

Cassie gently clasped his hand, which had tenderly caressed her face, and began, "Upon thorough investigation, we delved into the details of the accident."

JD anxiously inquired, "Did you get the other driver involved in the accident?"

Levi provided an update, stating, "The incident was hit-and-run. We're in the process of tracking down the driver using information gathered from witnesses. It's proving to be quite a challenging task."

JD nodded and thought he might pass out from the pain. "I'll work on it when I'm out of here."

Cassie added, "There's more to this."

JD felt the urge to raise his eyebrows in confusion, but the pain held him back. Instead, he opted to verbalize his inquiry, "What?"

Cassie's gaze shifted from Levi to JD as she began to speak. "Well, it's about the airbag—your side airbag, the one that didn't deploy—"

"Don't worry," JD said, "I'm going to sue them for enough to send Henry Kyle to college."

She glanced at Levi once more.

This time, Levi finally spoke up. "Based on the investigation findings, it was concluded that the equipment had been tampered with before the accident."

What? What was the man saying? "Tampered with?"

"Yeah," Cassie said, nodding thoughtfully. "We're in the process of figuring out who."

JD's mind raced with troubling thoughts. He couldn't help but wonder why someone would sabotage his airbag.

JD's mind was unable to cope with the subject any longer. He had not had the opportunity to inquire about his son. Thankfully, his son had not been in the truck. "Henry Kyle?"

Cassie gently released his hand and hesitated for a moment before speaking. "He's still at camp," she said softly. "I thought it was best for him to stay there while you were in the coma. I hope that's okay."

"That's perfect," JD thought as he looked at Cassie. Her caring treatment of Henry Kyle, as if he were her son, filled JD with gratitude and anticipation for their upcoming marriage.

"We were supposed to talk every night."

Cassie nodded slowly, her expression reflecting her understanding. "I know," she said with a thoughtful look. "I've been the one taking the calls."

JD shifted uncomfortably in his hospital gown, which was open in the rear, but at least he was covered in front.

"I've used excuses like you were on a case. I'm not sure he bought it, but he didn't push."

"Is he having fun?"

Cassie stood. "Based on what I've heard, he is. But he was concerned about you since he hadn't contacted you."

"Call the camp. I want to speak with him."

Cassie reached for JD's phone, her fingers tapping the screen as she scrolled through the list of recent calls to the camp and Mrs. Davis. With determination in her eyes, she selected a number and pressed the CALL button, the faint ringing tone echoing through the quiet room.

The phone rang for a few seconds, and Cassie hesitated before nearly deciding to hang up. However, just as she was about to end the call, someone finally answered.

"Hi," Cassie said pleasantly. "I'm looking for Mrs. Davis."

JD regretted Cassie not having used the speaker so that he could also listen to it.

"This is Cassie McKay. As Mrs. Davis knows, JD Walker has been in a coma and could not speak with his son. The doctor woke him today, and he wanted to speak with Henry Kyle. I know it's outside of calling hours—"

JD observed with concern as Cassie's complexion turned ashen, and her eyes widened with shock.

"Have you notified the police?"

What the hell? JD's heart pounded, and concern and confusion washed over him. Was something seriously wrong?

After a few "Okays," Cassie ended the call.

"What?" JD asked, his voice filled with fear as he awaited the answer. Was it about his son? His precious son?

She hesitated momentarily, and he felt the weight of her words in the air. With a deep breath, she finally spoke the sentence that would shatter him to the core.

"Henry Kyle is missing."

Chapter Fourteen

HENRY KYLE WOKE up suddenly, disoriented. He found himself in a car at a gas station, with Mrs. Davis pumping gas and smiling at him.

He strained to recollect the events leading up to his current situation. The only memory that surfaced was of sipping water from a bottle, but beyond that, everything was a blur. Could she have spiked his drink? No, that seemed farfetched. He reasoned that he was exhausted from the stress of his father's situation.

He realized he needed to piss, so he opened the door. "Are we almost there?" He couldn't believe he had fallen asleep while worrying about his dad. Why hadn't Miss Cassie told him his dad was hospitalized? Did she not think he was mature enough? That was unfair. Luckily, Mrs. Davis agreed to take him home.

Mrs. Davis nodded. "Sure are."

Relief washed over him as he felt the tension release from his heart and stomach. "I need to use the restroom," he said, clearing his throat. His dad mentioned that while men use the word "piss" between them, women aren't too keen on it.

Mrs. Davis's smile dropped. "Sure, there's one inside. Pick yourself up something to eat, and I'll be in in a minute to purchase the items."

Henry Kyle couldn't believe his luck in having Mrs. Davis help him. He didn't know how to react to Miss Cassie now that she had kept this secret from him.

He went to the back of the store and entered the restroom. Despite feeling dizzy, he leaned over the sink and splashed cool water on his face, attempting to ease his discomfort. After patting himself dry with a paper towel, he exited the cramped room and searched for snacks. His hunger persisted despite Mrs. Davis assuring him they were just about there. He felt grateful for her thoughtfulness in getting him something to eat.

As Henry Kyle reached for a bag of crispy potato chips and a tempting candy bar, he secretly hoped that she would indulge and buy both. Just as he was about to grab a soda, Mrs. Davis approached him from behind and gently reminded him, "We've got plenty of water in the car. It's better for you."

Since she'd denied the purchase, he closed the door and turned to her. "Are these snacks okay?" he asked, extending the munchies toward her.

"Those are fine. Let's pay for them. Then, we can get back on the road."

Henry Kyle stood at the checkout counter, carefully placing the items as Mrs. Davis prepared to pay. As he glanced around the shop, his eyes were drawn to a sign that proudly welcomed him to the small town. Suddenly, a wave of concern washed over him. This route took them toward Jackson, not home. His heart raced with worry as he frantically wondered if his dad's condition was indeed that dire.

He pondered whether they had airlifted him from Gulf Islands to the state capitol. With exhaustion still weighing him down, he closed his eyes briefly and swayed. Despite having already slept, he felt the urge to rest further. He should seize the opportunity to catch up on sleep during the car ride and keep himself awake to accompany his dad.

After settling the bill, he and Mrs. Davis returned to their car. With a warm smile, she passed him the bag of snacks, and he eagerly delved into the delicious treats.

As she prepared to leave, Henry Kyle politely requested, "Could I please have some water?"

Mrs. Davis turned towards him and flashed a warm smile. "Certainly, I'll grab one from the cooler," she chirped. Exiting the car, she walked to the trunk. Momentarily, she reappeared, carrying a chilled water bottle for Henry Kyle.

"Thank you," he said as he wiped the moisture from the ice on his shorts.

Once they hit the road, Henry Kyle found himself munching on snacks and water, his thoughts consumed by concern for his ailing father. The weariness from the journey began to weigh heavily on him, but amidst his drowsiness, lingering questions tugged at his mind. "How long has Dad been in the hospital?" Miss Cassie's words about his father being unavailable due to work commitments or stakeouts now appeared dubious, prompting Henry Kyle to ponder the veracity of her previous statements.

"A while," Mrs. David said softly.

Henry Kyle's veins pulsed with anger as he grappled with why Miss Cassie kept him from his dad. Did she truly desire his affection more than his son's? Though he didn't have the answer, the emotions roiling within him made it clear that he was troubled with her.

He had always been instructed to be honest, except for the rule about never telling a woman the truth when she asked how she looked. Other than that exception, he had been taught that there were no lies. However, Miss Cassie had deceived him.

As he sat there, a sudden thought pierced his mind like a bolt of lightning. He couldn't help but wonder why his father hadn't called him to come to the hospital. Was it possible that his father was replacing the love he should have received from Henry Kyle with Miss Cassie's care?

Too many questions and no answers. He'd have them soon enough, but that didn't stop him from wanting to know now. Henry Kyle rubbed his forehead.

"It must be a serious matter," he finally replied.

Mrs. David nodded. "I believe it is."

"Is that why we're going to Jackson? Was he airlifted there? Because only the worst cases are sent there."

Henry Kyle couldn't help but notice the shift in Mrs. Davis's demeanor. She stiffened and turned to look at him with a noticeable lack of a smile.

She quickly looked back at the road and inquired, "You're quite perceptive. How did you know we were heading to Jackson?"

Duh. "Where we stopped had a welcome sign."

Mrs. Davis pursed her lips. "Yes, we're headed to Jackson. Now, why don't you nap so you'll be refreshed for your father."

He had several more questions swirling in his mind. "What's the matter with my dad?" he asked. Strangely, he couldn't recall her providing this information, although she might have mentioned it when she initially informed him about his dad being admitted to the hospital. Everything that followed that moment seemed to be a complete blank.

"Sleep, Henry Kyle. All your questions will be answered soon."

Henry Kyle finished munching on his snacks and taking a few sips of water before leaning his head back in exasperation. Why were they keeping him in the dark? He may have only been ten—almost eleven, but he believed he was mature for his age, just as his dad always said.

He couldn't believe that everyone had kept this secret from him. He was torn about who he was most angry at. Should he be mad at his dad? Miss Cassie? Did Grandma Nan and Grandpa Gus have prior knowledge? The feeling of disappointment in his family was overwhelming.

As he slowly drifted off to sleep, he couldn't help but wonder about belonging to a family that trusted and treated him with absolute equality. In his mind's eye, he pictured a fairy godmother, whimsically granting him the fulfillment of this deeply cherished dream.

Chapter Fifteen

JD STRUGGLED WITH the IV in his right arm using his injured left hand, feeling a growing sense of frustration and anger as he found himself unable to remove the needle and finger monitor. "Get me the hell out of these things!"

"JD, no." Cassie quickly stepped forward to prevent him from harming himself while carefully removing the IV. Her desperate plea was filled with anguish as she uttered, "You just died last night. You can't get up yet. I can't have you die on me again."

Levi, with a stern look on his face, demanded, "Give me the phone."

Cassie wordlessly handed it over to Levi while maintaining her focus on JD.

As JD observed, Levi made his way to the corner of the room, speaking in low, secretive tones on his cell phone. He glanced at his watch a couple of times, clearly frustrated. *Damn it all to hell*. He should be the one to handle the essential calls, not get tangled up in these tubes.

Cassie gently held JD's hand and said, "JD, we'll find him. You need to recover." She stopped him as he tried to remove the needle from his hand.

"Cassie, if you think I'm going to sit here while my son is missing, you've lost your damn mind."

When Cassie stepped back, the agony was evident on her face. He realized he had spoken his mind. "I'm sorry, honey. What I meant was I must leave. I need to search for my son. I can't rely on anyone else to do it."

With a nod, she shifted her gaze toward Levi before pushing the call button for the nurse's station.

Levi ended the call and pivoted to face JD with a grave expression. "Here's the latest. Kerry, one of the workers, reported seeing Mrs. Davis and Henry Kyle departing from camp this morning."

"Did she fail to notify anyone?" JD bellowed angrily as the machines beeped, signaling an increase in his vitals. "That's a clear violation of camp protocol. And why on earth would my son agree to get in the car with her? He knows better than that."

Levi raised his shoulders in uncertainty. "We're still in the dark on that. She didn't reach out to anyone because Mrs. Davis is the boss, and she assumed the woman had special permission."

That angered JD even more. "Special permission, my ass," he exclaimed.

Cassie spoke in a soothing tone as she addressed him. "You must calm down, JD," she said. "Levi is trying to explain."

JD's hands attempted to clench into fists and failed as he battled the urge to lash out and hurl something across the room. His frustration at his inaction seethed through him, setting every nerve in his body on edge.

The nurse arrived, and JD declared, "I'm leaving, regardless of the doctor's approval."

The young nurse shook her blonde head in bewilderment.

Before the nurse could utter a word, Cassie explained the heart-wrenching news. "His son is missing."

The nurse's eyes widened as she abruptly ceased shaking her head and nodded in agreement. "I'll quickly check if the doctor is at the hospital," she stated before hastening away.

"I don't give a damn if the doctor is here or not. Now, Cassie, get me out of these things. I can't work the fingers on the left arm enough." He lifted his hand with the IV in the back of it. "Levi, call the FBI."

"Already dialing." Levi started to step into the hallway, and JD stopped him.

"No, keep the calls where I can hear."

Levi nodded, then swiftly sidestepped to avoid the bustling rush of hospital personnel flooding into the small room.

"Doc, I have to leave now!"

Dr. Myers's compassionate gaze met his, and she nodded. "The nurse has briefed me about your situation. Typically, I wouldn't advise it, but we are exploring the possibility of discharging you soon. We can manage your injuries on an outpatient basis."

Thank Christ. At least something was going right for him.

"But I expect you to watch for—"

Despite the doctor's warnings, JD brushed them off and sharply demanded, "Cassie, get me my clothes." Though he was aware of his being a demanding asshole, his desperation to find his son overshadowed any concern for politeness.

The intense, unbearable pain that had gripped his heart when Henry Kyle's mother had stolen him away years ago surged back into his consciousness with full force. The fear of losing his son once more overwhelmed him. During that time, he had plummeted into a profound abyss, and if it hadn't been for Gus and his supposed friends, he might have never found his way back to the surface.

JD observed Levi abruptly ending the call and immediately dialing another number. "What the hell?" He couldn't help but wonder why the FBI wouldn't offer to assist them in locating his son.

"Levi—"

Levi raised his index finger and pivoted away from JD, speaking in hushed tones that were inaudible to him. *Son of a bitch. This is my son. Mine!*

As Levi turned back to face him, JD felt a surge of anger, thinking that he might punch the man in the face for speaking too softly for him to hear. "What the hell, Levi?"

Unperplexed, Levi nodded. "The FBI, police, and CI team will meet us at the office in twenty minutes."

Twenty minutes felt excruciatingly long as JD contemplated the journey to Coastal Investigation. It was frustrating that his hometown lacked a proper hospital, being too small to support anything beyond a tiny urgent care clinic.

As Cassie stepped back, Levi returned to the phone while the nurse carefully released him from the hospital contraptions.

JD signed the paperwork and, with Cassie's assistance, dressed. When his head swam, he worried he might not be ready to leave the hospital. Then, he thought of his son and didn't care. Even on his deathbed, he'd find Henry Kyle. And, apparently, he'd been there already.

In around twenty minutes, the three reached CI. As they arrived, they found the FBI, police, and CI team all positioned and ready. Nan had thoughtfully prepared freshly brewed coffee, and someone—probably Daisy— had grabbed a selection of sandwiches.

JD's stomach twisted with worry as he realized it was already lunchtime. His son had been gone for far too long, and the anxiety gnawed at him like a relentless predator.

FBI Special Agent Miranda Miles presented her new partner—Special Agent Ryker Evans. The pair would now take charge of the complex investigation into the disappearance of a child that crossed state lines. Henry Kyle's kidnapping fell outside of his hometown's usual jurisdiction, leading Gulf Islands Police Chief Buster Cox to insist on being involved in all meetings and updates, as Henry was one of his citizens.

Gus slapped JD on the shoulder, causing a wince of pain. "We git da boy back."

Everyone gathered around the table in the central area, pulling up chairs to fit into the space.

Agent Miles commenced the meeting by stating, "Here's what we know. At approximately 9:30 a.m., Irene Davis took Henry Kyle from his camp. Kerry White, a volunteer, witnessed them entering Mrs. Davis's car."

"We already know this," JD slammed his hand on the table in frustration, his voice coated with urgency and determination. He wanted to find his son, not waste time rehashing information they already knew. The need to hit the streets to search for Henry Kyle weighed heavily on his mind, while he needed Levi to get to his computer and meticulously track down traffic cams.

"What we've since found out," FBI Special Agent Miles continued as if JD hadn't exploded, "is that Irene Davis is an alias."

JD was overcome with a sudden and overwhelming fear, which halted his rage in its tracks. His mind and body were consumed by the incomprehensible idea that someone would go to such extreme measures to kidnap his son. He was baffled by the absence of ransom demand, deepening the dread and confusion.

The realization left him with just one conclusion: the kidnapper had no intention of bringing Henry Kyle back home.

JD rested his head in his right hand, taking a moment to compose himself. With assistance from this group, he was determined to find his son.

JD straightened his back, feeling on edge as he uttered, "Go on." He braced himself to listen, aware that the FBI had already thoroughly investigated the kidnapper's background.

"We've sent a forensic team from the New Orleans field office to take fingerprints from her office to see if we can identify her. In the interim, JD, you must keep your phone line open for a potential ransom demand. We'll discuss with you how to answer the call, etc."

JD double-checked his phone multiple times to ensure he hadn't missed any calls.

"Here's what—"

The piercing and abrupt ring of JD's cell phone interrupted FBI Special Agent Miles, causing an immediate and tense silence to fall over everyone in the room.

Chapter Sixteen

WITH TREMBLING HANDS, JD reached for his cell phone. A sense of dread enveloped him. Was it the kidnapper or a law enforcement agency calling to inform him of his son's demise? Both options left him feeling helpless.

He ended the call abruptly, feeling the weight of the phone in his hand as he let it slip through his fingers. "Bryant," he muttered, the taste of bitterness tainting the name on his lips. Once a friend, now a legal representative, JD grappled with a lack of desire to converse with the man.

JD shook his head slightly and gestured for Agent Miles to continue. "Go on," he urged.

As the agent was about to continue, JD's phone rang again, breaking the tense atmosphere. With his heart pounding and nerves on edge, he quickly reached for the phone. It was Bryant calling again.

Their childhood pact was that if either of them called twice, something urgent required attention. Holding true to this understanding, JD responded to the second call. Irritated, he growled, "What?"

"Vince's mom is missing."

His feelings towards Vince's mom remained unchanged, regardless of the troubles Vince had caused him. Now, finding Henry Kyle was his primary concern. "I'm sorry, Bryant. I have bigger issues to deal with. My son is missing," he said before ending the call.

Agent Miles said without being prompted, "As I was saying, as soon as we get the prints back to the lab, we'll see what we've got."

"And if the prints produce nothing?" JD asked.

"We also have a BOLO out on her car." Agent Miles looked at her notes.

Agent Evans recited the Mississippi license plate number for a Blue Hyundai Sonata before his partner could speak.

JD struggled to recall anyone he knew who owned a Blue Sonata and had malicious intentions toward him. He wracked his brain, but no one came to mind.

"Enough. If we don't know anything yet, I'm driving to the camp and see for myself."

Cassie lightly touched his arm and looked at him. "I'll drive you."

"There's no need," Agent Miles responded.

JD's gaze remained fixed on Agent Miles, his expression intense and nonwavering.

The tired agent let out a heavy sigh, indicating her resignation. JD interpreted this as a sign that she knew he would not be dissuaded. "Fine. We'll meet you there," she responded.

JD did his best to get comfortable in Cassie's Jeep, but the pain in his arm and labored breathing made it difficult. Nevertheless, they sped after the agents to the camp.

As JD stood at the Louisiana camp, memories of dropping off Henry Kyle came flooding back. He vividly recalled the mix of excitement and nerves on his son's face, knowing that this camp experience was utterly new to him. Henry Kyle, being homeschooled, didn't have any friends attending, intensifying JD's sense of guilt. He regretted not thoroughly researching the camp before enrolling his son. The glossy brochure, enticing website, and his son's eager anticipation of a "normal" experience had clouded his judgment.

The boy had experienced anything but an ordinary life before coming to live with JD. His journey to JD's home began tragically following the murder of his mother, leaving JD constantly feeling for the child when he reflected on the difficult start to his life.

"Hi, I'm Kerry." As JD observed the young volunteer, he pondered whether the teenager could be relied upon to recall all the details she had described accurately. It was evident that she harbored animosity towards her camp leader. This raised the question of whether she was embellishing her account to portray the leader in a negative light when, in reality, the camp may have been negligent.

JD cut straight to the point, demanding without pleasantries, "Tell me what happened?"

Kerry gently pushed a loose strand of hair behind her ear, her solemn gaze sweeping across the group. "Like I told the other agents, Mrs. Davis took Henry Kyle in her car around 9:30 this morning. She hadn't returned since.

JD squinted at his watch. Three o'clock. An exasperated tone seeped into his question as he ground out, "What took so long to report it?"

The volunteer jumped at his harsh tone. "I— I reported it at eleven when they didn't return for the meal. I expected she would be back."

"Isn't it against the rules to drive a kid in your personal vehicle?"

"Well, yes." The girl moved from side to side, nervousness in her voice.

JD advanced threateningly on the girl. "And that didn't make you think something was wrong?"

Cassie grabbed his good arm before he could do something unwise. "JD."

He became acutely aware of his impact on the girl when Cassie touched him. With a heavy sigh, he ran his hand over his face and spoke softly, "I'm sorry."

"I did get the tag number," the girl said in a feeble attempt to salvage herself.

"That was a good idea," Cassie said with encouragement. "But why did you get the tag number if you felt nothing was wrong?"

The young girl's eyes widened, resembling a deer frozen in the glare of headlights. Kerry nonchalantly shrugged and said, "I don't know. I seem to have a talent for remembering what I see, and I noticed the license plate as they drove away."

Agent Miles demanded, taking charge of the interrogation and asking, "Which way did they go?"

Kerry gestured with her shaking arm in the direction of the northeast.

By this time of the day, they could be anywhere in Louisiana or Mississippi. JD's mind raced with questions about the mysterious Mrs. Davis or whatever her real name might be. Where could she be heading? But the most pressing question that weighed on his mind was why an older woman would be interested in his son.

JD anxiously glanced at his phone again, hoping he hadn't missed a call. Bryant's message about Vince's mom needing to talk weighed on his mind. Despite his regret, JD knew he couldn't afford to divert his attention to her at this moment.

A well-dressed man, his attire suggesting he may be an FBI agent, briskly approached them. "They've been sighted off I-59 in Hattiesburg."

People may get lost in a college town if they intend to stay there permanently.

After the agent provided the gas station location, JD decisively broke away from the group, indifferent to whether anyone accompanied them except Cassie. Their sole focus was to reach the gas station and access the security footage.

"JD, stop," Agent Miles said in a sharp tone.

JD kept moving forward, but his surprise grew as Agent Evans appeared beside him. Damn, that man was fast. Perhaps he was past special forces.

Agent Miles raised her voice for him to hear. "If you'd have some patience, we're having the feed emailed to us."

Agent Miles just became his favorite friend.

JD was not known for his patience, especially during this particular situation. He struggled with it even when his son wasn't missing.

Cassie gently rested her hand on his back, offering silent support and comfort. "Are you in pain?"

Physically and mentally drained, he shook his head. "I'm fine," he said, although he struggled to believe it himself. At that moment, he knew he had to redirect his focus to Henry Kyle.

Holding Cassie close, JD embraced her tenderly, mindful of his injuries. As he drew strength from her, he maintained his composure, yet the weight of the possibility of losing his son was almost too much to bear. "I want him back."

"I know, sweetheart. We'll get him back."

"I can't lose him, Cassie." His voice broke as he spoke her name.

She gently lifted her head from his shoulder and fixed her gaze on him, meeting his eyes. "You won't. Now, don't even think like that. We've got the FBI looking for him, and they already have a few clues, plus a security tape coming. We're going to find him, JD."

"JD," Agent Evans said, breaking into their conversation. "The video is here. Come see if you recognize this woman."

Why was he nervous? JD feared encountering his son tied up and couldn't handle it all. He hoped the kidnapper wouldn't cause more mental anguish for Henry Kyle.

JD nodded, eager to watch the video. However, he was disappointed to find that it was grainy. He wondered why people still employed those old video cameras when newer ones provided crisper pictures. Didn't they want to catch thieves and vandals?

JD noticed something that caught his eye, causing his heart to lurch. "Play it again."

After watching it for the second time, he exploded in anger. JD angrily dialed a number on his phone and demanded, "Why didn't you tell me?"

Bryant said, "I tried."

Chapter Seventeen

AN AIR OF frenzied activity enveloped Cassie and JD as they found themselves surrounded by a sense of urgency. Despite her eagerness to assist, Cassie felt hampered by the fact that the FBI held the reins of the investigation. The FBI swiftly disseminated a photo of Mrs. Vivian St. Amant and her license plate number to their agents and the media. The pressing need to locate Henry Kyle weighed heavily on everyone involved.

JD gripped Cassie's upper arm and whispered, "Come." They avoided the commotion and halted at Cassie's Jeep.

She turned to him, locking her gaze with his. "What's up?" she inquired with a curious tilt of her head.

"We need to get out of here and find my son."

"But—"

JD's jaw clenched tightly, the muscles visibly twitching with tension. "These pricks couldn't find their ass from a hole in the ground. If anyone is going to find my son, it will have to be us."

Cassie felt a sense of uncertainty creeping in, but she was acutely aware of the pressing need to assist in some way. "Where do we start?"

"We need Levi—"

A sleek, black Jacquar came to a sudden stop behind the Jeep.

"Son of a bitch," JD muttered.

Cassie shifted her attention to the newcomer, Bryant Jacobs, who emerged from the sportscar wearing jeans and a blue button-down shirt, sleeves rolled to his elbows.

She observed JD as he folded his arm over his broken arm across his chest, shutting himself off. Her heart ached for him as she considered the deep rift that had formed between two men who had been close friends for most of their lives. Would JD find it in his heart to forgive Bryant?

"What the hell do you want? Are you here to sleep with my girlfriend?" JD said with disdain dripping from his voice.

Okay, the chances of them reconciling today seemed slim.

"I want to help." Bryant turned to Cassie. "Hello, Cassie. It's good to see you."

She hesitated, unsure whether to speak, and instead nodded to him. She was reluctant to give Bryant any advantage in their ongoing struggle.

JD grabbed her hand and pulled her toward him in an immature move. "I don't need your help."

"You need everyone's help. Now, I don't care if you like me, but that is my godson, and by all that's holy, I will bring him home."

"He's no longer your godson."

"JD, I'm not going to argue with you now. Where are you with finding Henry Kyle, and how can I help in the search?"

Cassie observed JD's demeanor shift several times until he decided Henry Kyle's safety outweighed their ongoing feud.

Much to her surprise, JD exclaimed, "Okay, we're making our way to where they were last seen."

"Do you want me to ride along?" Bryant asked.

JD immediately expelled, "No."

"JD, dammit, I need to help."

"And you will. Go to CI and help Levi. You have contacts that may help in the search."

Bryant thoughtfully nodded. "I can do that. Anything else?"

JD narrowed his eyes at his old friend. "Yeah, stay away from Cassie."

Cassie's jaw tightened as it became her turn to react. Despite the urge to express that she could take care of herself, and that Bryant posed no threat, she could see that JD was in pain and needed to voice his concerns. She decided to let him speak for now, but she seethed with the knowledge that she would confront him later.

With a nod, Bryant turned on his heel and returned to his sleek sports car. As he revved the engine, he left in a hurry, leaving behind a cloud of dust that filled the air.

"Come on," JD said, full of urgency. "Let's get on the road. I'll call Levi while you drive."

"Aren't we going to tell the FBI we're leaving?"

JD gazed at the agents swarming the scene and said, "No."

Once they got into the Jeep, they left the camp and headed toward the interstate.

JD dialed Levi's number and put the phone on speaker. Cassie felt a sense of relief as she sat in the Jeep with the top on, knowing they were expecting a storm. However, she couldn't shake off the worry that they might encounter it during their drive.

"Levi—" JD began but was cut off by his colleague.

"Already on it. I'm texting the address and witness name for the gas station on I-59."

CI was fortunate to have Levi, and JD felt thankful that Levi was already working on the case. Nothing the FBI—or former FBI—disliked more than missing children.

"The witness stated they returned to the interstate heading north. No traffic cams or tolls exist in that area, so I'm blind right now. Although I've put a patch to my computer, we will if the FBI finds anything."

"Um," Cassie hesitated, "Isn't that illegal?"

Levi scoffed as he uttered, "Who cares? Henry Kyle is missing. I would do anything to find that boy. I'm not concerned about the FBI figuring this out before I act."

"Enough," JD exclaimed, frustration evident in his voice. "How on earth are we supposed to find him without cameras? They could have traveled a significant distance with a full gas tank."

"Don't worry," Levi assured him. "I'm combing through Mrs. St Amant's life to see if she has relations up north or anything to tie to her."

"Get over to her place before the FBI and see what clues you can find." A call beeped in on JD's phone. "Damn, FBI." He sent the call to voicemail.

"Gus and Nan are already there. They haven't found anything yet but give them time."

JD slammed his good hand on the dashboard. "Dammit, we don't have time. There's no telling what she's doing to my son. The kidnapping must be payback for killing her son."

"JD," Cassie attempted to soothe, "don't worry. We'll find him soon. The gas station said Henry Kyle was well, so keep that in mind."

He closed his eyes. "I know." He opened them and added, pleading in them. "I just can't lose him."

Cassie reached over and gently clasped his hand, her expression filled with determination as she reassured him, "We won't."

He squeezed her hand, gazed at her, and smiled brightly. "You're right. We." Returning to the call, he said, "Levi, Bryant is heading your way. He's been around Mrs. St. Amant more than I have. He may have some clues. Use him."

"Sure thing."

They ended the call.

JD leaned back in his seat and closed his eyes. "This is my worst nightmare come true," he whispered, the weight of his words hanging heavily in the air.

Cassie flipped the switch to activate the windshield wipers as the rain poured. Up ahead, she noticed the looming dark clouds of an intense storm. They were driving straight into it. Maybe the storm was causing Henry Kyle's abductor to slow down or even halt.

"Call Levi back," Cassie directed with a thought.

Turning to her, JD asked, "What for?"

"Just do it."

Putting the phone on speaker, JD let out a heavy sigh, the weariness evident in his voice. "This weather sucks."

"Exactly."

"Yeah," Levi answered.

"Levi," Cassie said with urgency, "there's a big storm in the area where Mrs. St. Amant was traveling. Check the rest stops and any place before Jackson. They wouldn't have made it that far without the need to slow down driving."

"On it." Levi clicked off the call with more excitement in his voice than when he'd answered.

"Do you really think she'll have stopped?"

Cassie nodded her certainty. "I do. That storm has been in the area all morning. Ahead, it's pouring so hard we won't be able to see ahead. We'll need to slow down significantly. So would she have."

"Yeah, but that doesn't get us closer to her. Why do you think she'd stop?"

"Because Henry Kyle is a smart boy. He'll try to get her somewhere we can find them, or he can escape."

JD's phone rang from an unknown number, creating tension and fear that radiated in the cab.

Chapter Eighteen

DESPERATELY, HENRY KYLE whispered into the stranger's borrowed cell phone, urging someone to answer. The man in the restroom had graciously offered him the use of his phone. Henry Kyle longed to convey that he had been kidnapped, but Mrs. Davis had threatened to kill his dad if he revealed anything. He couldn't bear the thought of her harming his father.

He suddenly became aware that she had been drugging him with the water, causing him to refuse any more of it. He insisted that he had to use the restroom before thinking about taking another sip. Given the stormy weather, they stopped at a run-down gas station off the main road in Laurel.

Someone picked up the call but remained silent.

"Dad?"

"Champ!" He could hear the fear in his dad's voice. "Are you okay? Where are you?"

Relief at finally speaking with someone who could help surged through him. His dad would rescue him, he knew.

"I'm in—"

As he was about to speak, Mrs. Davis burst into the men's room, brandishing a gun and aiming it at him and the man who had lent him the phone.

"Hang up," his abductor said.

The man pushed Henry Kyle behind him for protection. "Wait a minute. Put the gun down. There's no need for violence."

Henry Kyle could hardly hear the dull thud of the shot. He watched in shock as the man standing in front of him crumpled to the floor, blood seeping onto the dirty tile. When he turned to look at Mrs. Davis, he noticed the gun in her hand was fitted with one of those suppressor attachments that he had only ever seen in movies. It struck him as odd. Weren't those suppressors illegal? But then again, everything about Mrs. Davis's actions seemed to be outside the bounds of the law.

"I said, hang up."

Henry Kyle reluctantly followed the orders, torn between the fear of getting shot and the dread of facing possible death. He found relief in the thought that at least his father would be reassured of his safety. With Mr. Levi's exceptional intelligence and computer expertise, Henry hoped he could trace the call as they did in the movies.

Mrs. Davis waved the gun toward the door. "Let's go."

Henry Kyle's heart raced as he emerged from the restroom, the lingering unease evident in his hurried steps. Would she shoot him in the back? Absolute terror suddenly engulfed his entire being for the very first time.

A sinking disappointment settled in as Henry Kyle scanned the desolate parking lot. No car except the lone vehicle parked in front of the restroom could be seen. To add to his unease, the clerk's absence inside the store made the prospect of escape seem increasingly bleak.

Back in the vehicle, Mrs. Davis handed him a tainted water. "Drink."

"I don't want to be drugged any longer."

"I don't care what you want. You will drink this, or I will pour it down your throat."

Faced with the threat of a gun in her hands, Henry Kyle hesitated to voice his objections, knowing that she was capable of using it. Instead, he reluctantly decided to drink the tainted water, feeling that being drugged was a better alternative to facing the barrel of her gun.

After a short while, he began to feel a strong wave of drowsiness sweeping over him.

****

"Levi, trace the damn call," JD growled, his voice edged with fear and urgency. A chill shot through him as he registered the suppressed gunshot he had just heard. Had Mrs. St. Amant shot Henry Kyle? The thought of his son being wounded or, even worse, dead was unbearable. JD refused to accept the latter, but even the possibility of Henry being wounded meant serious trouble for his son.

"Okay, I've got the general area…."

"Levi—" JD started, but Levi continued.

"Okay, around the area where the call was made are two gas stations. Although, from what I can tell, you're looking for the second one." He provided a name and address.

JD carefully input the address into the GPS on the Jeep's central console.

As they continued along I-59 instead of turning north, JD couldn't help but wonder about their destination. The idea of an unplanned kidnapping crossed his mind, and he struggled with the unsettling thought of the woman doing something reckless.

JD longed for the relentless storm to let up, yearning for Cassie to accelerate, but he found comfort in realizing that Mrs. St. Amant's movements were also hindered. The need to see his son, wrap him in his arms, and ensure his well-being weighed heavily on JD, driving his fervent wish for them to hasten their pace and catch up.

"JD," Bryant interjected on the call on Cassie's car speaker. "Do you remember the summer when we were eight and went camping? Only your dad wouldn't allow you to go?"

Why on earth was Bryant dredging up that painful memory at this moment? JD vividly recalled his excitement about a trip with his friends. Despite having access to a cabin, they had decided to rough it by camping in the backyard. Suddenly, a realization struck him like a bolt of lightning—the cabin.

"Where is it?"

"I'm not certain, but I know it's in Meridian."

"Levi," JD growled, "I thought you told us she didn't own any other properties."

"She doesn't."

JD furrowed his brow, deep in thought. He felt there must be something he had overlooked. "Search under her deceased husband's name. Look in Vince's name, too. Perhaps she never changed the title after they both passed away."

"I'm checking under Henry St. Amant," Levi advised over the sound of keys clicking on a keyboard.

Before JD could speak, Bryant said, "I think it's under Vince's name. Vince mentioned getting property after his father died. I never inquired what since he always boasted of being so wealthy."

"Nothing under Henry St. Amant," Levi said before adding, "Checking Vincent St. Amant."

The answer seemed to take an eternity to arrive, but surprisingly, it came swiftly and without delay.

"Bingo," Levi said with excitement. "Vince owns property in Meridian. I'll text you the address and send it to the FBI."

JD hesitated, cautioning against immediate contact with the FBI. He felt torn between the necessity of alerting them and the dread of a potentially hazardous response, such as a reckless ambush that could endanger his son. With Mrs. St. Amant armed and ready, JD couldn't afford to risk any missteps.

"Don't send it to the FBI yet."

"All right," Levi said with reluctance, especially considering he was still with the FBI. "You tell me when to share."

The call abruptly ended, leaving JD feeling uneasy. Within moments, his phone rang again, signaling the FBI's relentless pursuit of him. Frustrated, he weighed his options before reluctantly deciding to answer to shake them off his trail.

"Walker."

"JD," Agent Miles barked, "where are you?"

"I'm on the road." As if he would actually disclose his location to them.

"We can't have you interfering in this investigation. Leave it to the professionals."

Professionals, my ass.

"I'm not interfering. We're just out for a drive."

"To a small gas station in Hattiesburg?" Agent Miles asked.

Upon disregarding the witness, JD found lying unnecessary and proceeded directly to the cabin. "No, ma'am. We're not headed to Hattiesburg."

"See that you keep it that way."

"Is that all?"

"No. I called to tell you someone responded to the Amber Alert at a small gas station in Laurel."

It must be the man JD overheard who had bravely defended his son.

"I'm sorry to tell you that Mrs. St. Amant has a weapon and has already shot one person."

He felt a surge of relief as he realized that even though Mrs. St. Amant had shot someone, it meant that Henry Kyle had not been harmed despite feeling terrible about the situation; knowing that Henry was safe provided a sense of immense relief.

"Okay."

"Okay? Is that all? I tell you a man has been shot, and your son's abductor is armed, and all you can say is 'okay?'"

JD realized that this was a test to gauge his knowledge and suspicions. "There's nothing I can do about it, right? So, 'okay,'" he said. He had to tell her, even though she already knew, but for some reason, she left it to him to disclose. "Henry Kyle called me."

"We know. What did he say?"

"He didn't get anything more than 'Dad' out?"

"Why didn't you call us?"

"I planned to do that."

"And? What stopped you?"

"Look, Agent Miles. Just get my son back. If something happens to him—" JD choked up at the vision and couldn't complete the sentence. "Just find him."

"We will. I'll call you with any updates. I expect you to do the same."

JD ended the call, feeling a sense of urgency to reach the cabin. As he contemplated the situation, he fervently prayed—yes, prayed—that the cabin was indeed Mrs. St. Amant's intended destination. Otherwise, it would mean precious time wasted.

"Can you pick up the pace?" he urged Cassie. They were rushing to reach their destination, and he feared what the woman might do with his son once they arrived.

"Don't you dare take your mood out on me. I'm going faster than I should in this weather."

JD dropped his head and sighed heavily. "I'm sorry, sweetheart. I'm just—"

"I know. It's okay. How are your arm and head?"

The man found it amusing that he had not been aware of his pain until she brought it up. With his complete attention on his son, his discomfort seemed to vanish.

"They're fine."

"Liar."

So, he was. "You got me. But they're nothing to the pain in my gut. It's my fault my son has been kidnapped." On that momentous day, both he and Cassie had aimed at Vince. However, his single shot had tragically resulted in the death of his friend.

If a tragedy befell Henry Kyle, he couldn't fathom how he would continue living with the weight of responsibility on his shoulders. Even the comforting presence of Cassie wouldn't be sufficient to ease his burden. The gnawing guilt was taking a toll on him, and he feared it would only intensify if—

"Stop thinking like that," Cassie said firmly but with compassion.

How had she known what he'd been thinking?

"We're going to get him back," she assured him.

JD knew that, but the looming question remained: would it be dead or alive?

Chapter Nineteen

AS I PULL up to the secluded cabin, a rush of relief washes over me. I'm glad I didn't change the ownership from Vince's name. The stirrings of my grandson prompted me to consider our next move. We can only afford a brief respite here before hitting the road again. I know that the FBI or JD will eventually catch wind of Vince's property, so our stay here can only be temporary.

I don't know how much time we have before they find us. I refuse to let them separate me from Henry Kyle. If they try to do it, it will be time for Henry Kyle and me to reunite with the boy's late father in the afterlife. I long for Vince deeply.

I was sure an Amber Alert was issued for my grandson, along with a description of my car. Fortunately, I had taken some old license plates from other vehicles that looked like mine in the grocery store parking lot. It was a relief to have something that wouldn't attract attention.

"Mrs. Davis?" Henry Kyle questioned as he groggily woke. "Where are we?"

As I gaze at the boy, a warm smile spreads inside me. His resemblance to my son Vincent is striking. Some might say he looks like JD, but those comments are merely courtesy.

"We're taking a nap here."

Henry Kyle yawned and stretched. "I've already taken a nap."

Oh, you'll take another one before the day is done. "I need a nap." It would be a long night planning their subsequent move.

****

Fully conscious and alert, Henry Kyle jolted as he realized he was still in this desperate situation. It hadn't been a figment of his imagination. The memory of Mrs. Davis firing the gun at a man who had loaned him the phone sent shivers down his spine. He couldn't help but worry about the man's well-being. The thought of being indirectly responsible for someone's death was unbearable to him.

As he thought about his predicament, he remembered being coerced by the woman to drink spiked water and being threatened with a gunshot if he tried to escape. He realized it was up to him to find a way out, knowing that his father and Miss Cassie would not know where to look for him.

Henry Kyle glanced around, trying to get his bearings. "Should I keep watch while you nap?" he asked, his voice barely above a whisper. Perhaps if she felt reassured, she would drift off to sleep, giving him the chance to slip away.

She laughed, sending shivers down his spine. "You're a bright child, but no. You will also sleep."

"But, Mrs. Davis, I've already slept most of the day."

"Stop calling me that," she snapped, her voice tinged with annoyance. "To you, my name is 'Grandma.'"

"Like Grandma Nan?" Henry Kyle was puzzled by her request to be called "Grandma." Although elderly, she didn't seem old enough to be called that.

"No, like your real grandmother. My name is Vivian St. Amant, and you, precious boy, are my son Vincent's boy."

Henry Kyle struggled to comprehend her peculiar behavior. She appeared to be loonier than anyone he had encountered before. It was evident to him, as JD Walker's son, that her craziness surpassed that of anyone else he knew.

"I can see you don't believe me."

Nope, he didn't. He sat frozen in place, not making a single movement, as he desperately wished for this absurd conversation to end.

"Let's go inside," she said with a wave.

Henry Kyle nonchalantly raised his shoulders in a resigned gesture, fully aware that he was at the mercy of the situation, with the woman wielding a gun while he had nothing but his wits to rely on.

****

Their terrible luck angered JD. A significant accident had closed their side of the interstate for miles. They felt fortunate not to have been involved in the accident, especially as the car behind them had skidded to a stop just inches from Cassie's bumper.

"What should we do next?" she inquired with a furrowed brow, her voice tinged with uncertainty.

He was filled with unwavering determination. He vowed to find his son and bring him to safety, no matter what it took. "Switch the radio to the traffic broadcast. We need to know what's going on," he instructed, urgency coloring his every word.

With a confident smile, Cassie announced, "I have a better idea," as she pulled the hood of her raincoat over her head and stepped out of the Jeep, ready to take charge.

JD was alarmed and almost leaped out of the vehicle, but he hesitated, realizing that someone should stay with the running Jeep. Although he could turn off the engine and follow, he had to trust Cassie to handle the situation. He knew he had to come up with a plan.

While Cassie consulted with a commercial truck driver, JD called Levi for assistance. "Can you get me a helicopter?"

"Whoa. I can do many things, but I'm not sure about that. Although I know where one can be found to find your son, you can't be on it."

JD let out a heavy groan, realizing that he would have to relinquish control to the FBI. However, he was determined to be present when his son was rescued.

Cassie bounded back into the Jeep, and with a concerned expression, she informed him, "The accident is five miles in front of us. They've almost cleared it, but we have five miles of backed-up traffic ahead."

Son of a bitch! "Go ahead and call them." He ended the call.

Cassie reached to touch his thigh. "Are you going to turn this over?"

"I have to. I can't let that crazy woman have him longer than necessary." As he settled back into the seat, he felt the weight of his emotions pressing against his closed eyelids, holding back tears that begged to escape. The thought of losing Henry Kyle, the boy who held his heart, was intolerable.

"I guess this means we're not getting married in a couple of weeks then," Cassie said to lighten the mood.

Crap. His mind had not wandered to their wedding since the incident occurred. It was as if the thought of it had been locked away until this was all behind him. "I don't know."

Hesitantly, Cassie asked, "Is that an I don't know to a couple of weeks or an I don't know at all?"

"I just don't know," he admitted. He felt a pressing need to focus all his attention on Henry Kyle, especially after who knew what the vile woman had told his son. They faced obstacles and would likely have to work on rebuilding their relationship as father and son. At that moment, nothing else mattered, not even his job at CI or Cassie.

"I just don't know."

Chapter Twenty

STUNNED AND OVERWHELMED by the situation, Cassie found herself back amid the stalled traffic, unable to proceed with the efforts to rescue Henry Kyle. The words "I just don't know" echoed repeatedly in her mind, reflecting her uncertainty and confusion. She grappled with the decision to allow JD to focus on finding his missing son, even though it meant putting their wedding on hold. How JD responded with that statement to her question added another layer of complexity to an already tense and emotional situation.

She adored Henry Kyle as if he were her son. At present, he was her top priority. However, she felt it was essential for JD to divert his thoughts and unwind. He was agitated and required some alternate perspectives to assist him in resetting his mindset about his son's abduction. They needed to revisit the initial stages of the situation.

As the traffic slowly inched forward, Cassie was inching along with it. It seemed like they couldn't leave this chaotic situation until it nearly dark. All the while, she couldn't shake the feeling that the FBI, the very organization it killed JD to contact, was already at the cabin. She feared they would have removed any evidence that could have aided her and JD in their quest to find Henry Kyle.

"Why do you think she's doing this now?" Cassie questioned as she glanced into the right lane, slowly inching forward. Determined, she skillfully maneuvered between two vehicles. No matter what, they would escape this situation, even if she had to take the off-road route.

JD wiped his hand wearily down his face, indicating his distress. "I have a feeling that she's been wanting custody of him since Vince's passing."

This new information took Cassie aback. The fact that he hadn't shared it with her hurt her deeply. It made her ponder whether he had been showing signs of withdrawal even before the abduction. Despite her desire to delve into their relationship dynamics, she knew that finding Henry Kyle was the top priority at that moment.

"Oh?" Cassie turned on her turn signal and guided the Jeep toward another lane.

"He's letting you over."

As Cassie switched to the adjacent lane, a sigh of relief escaped her as she noticed they were now traveling at least twenty miles per hour. This indicated that the roads must have been cleared of the crash.

"Yeah. It's crap. I've just ignored the anonymous threats. Which is probably why she went to this extreme."

Cassie would wholeheartedly agree with that conclusion. "Does she have the funds to continue to run?"

JD exhaled a loud, deep breath. "Yes."

Growing up, Vince had always been known as the "rich kid." However, Cassie had no idea if Mrs. St. Amant had managed to maintain that wealth. It was apparent that she had, which wasn't a promising sign for their pursuit if she continued evading them.

JD's phone rang, and he gruffly answered it with, "Yeah?"

Cassie fixed her eyes on the road, determined to block out the one-sided conversation likely to lead to more questions than answers.

"It was Henry Kyle. I'm sure of it."

Cassie was immediately intrigued by what she heard. She longed for him to put the phone on speaker, as he had previously done. His tendency to keep things to himself differed from how she envisioned their relationship progressing.

"We're changing direction. Keep me updated, Levi." JD turned to her with excitement shown in his eyes. "We're headed to Oxford."

"Why Oxford? That's so far out of the way."

"Because she's taking Henry Kyle there."

That was enough for Cassie to reroute their trip in her GPS. "How do they—I'm assuming the FBI—know they're running to Oxford?"

Proudly, JD boasted, "My brilliant son. He wrote 'Oxford' in the dirt outside the cabin."

Way to go, Henry Kyle. "It'll take us a while to get there. Do we know where once we're in Oxford?"

"No, but the Memphis airport is close, so we need to move faster."

Cassie turned to him, ready to snap. "How do you expect me to do that? Run over the cars in front of me?" She hadn't meant to be curt with him, but he'd irked her.

"I'm sorry, Cassie. I know you're doing the best you can. I just need to get there."

"I get that. And we will. We'll jump off at the next exit and take an alternate route."

"That's my girl."

Cassie felt a flutter in her stomach when he called her that. It helped her push aside her worries about their situation. "Do we know anyone up that way who could help us?" She tried to think of old college friends who might have settled there but couldn't think of anyone.

JD scrolled through his contacts on his phone and said, "No. It's time to call in help, though."

"What kind of help?" If the person wasn't currently in Oxford already, it didn't matter. They needed someone locally to find Henry Kyle's location.

"Don't worry." He put the phone to his ear and shut her out. "Hey bud, it's JD Walker."

She could not guess the identity of the man he was conversing with, but she was confident it was a man. Perhaps he was acquainted with someone in Memphis, conveniently located just an hour from Oxford. Additionally, her thoughts were preoccupied with the airport. It was worth noting that there was a private airport in Oxford, commonly utilized by individuals flying in for the Ole Miss games.

"My son has been abducted."

As Cassie listened to him recount the events following Henry Kyle's disappearance, she couldn't help but notice the tremble in his voice. She longed to comfort him and promised that everything would work out. It seemed that Mrs. St. Amant didn't seek to harm Henry Kyle but instead wanted to keep him exclusively for herself.

JD checked his watch and passed along their arrival time from the GPS. "Where will I find you?"

That's good. Someone else will assist. They'll be in Oxford first. Finally, things were going in their favor.

Cassie felt the urge to call Levi for an update as she had only heard one side of JD's conversation, and he hadn't shared the rest. However, she knew that reaching out to Levi would only upset JD. Hence, she decided to wait until JD was ready to divulge the details.

"Great. I'll see you there. Thanks, bud. I owe you big time." After concluding the call, JD leaned back in his seat with a heavy sigh.

Finally, Cassie exited the interstate and eased into a nearby gas station to refuel. Once she parked at the pump, she turned to JD and firmly said, "Tell me what's been happening." She was determined not to be sidelined and only serve as a chauffeur.

So, JD provided her with an update. The main point was that the FBI had missed Henry Kyle at the cabin, but evidence showed it had been recently occupied. The writing in the dirt appeared fresh, suggesting that Henry Kyle had managed to send them a message. Cassie felt a surge of pride for the boy's resourcefulness and quick thinking.

"What about the person you just called? Is someone else helping?" She deserved to know if they were partnering with one another.

"Yes. An old FBI friend."

"I thought you hated everyone in the FBI."

"Not this one. He came down on a case I worked on and actually worked with me instead of ramrodding me."

"If he's FBI, how can he interfere? Won't Agent Miles kick him to the curb?" She couldn't fathom the idea of the FBI permitting another agent to infringe on the investigation. Still, given the severity of the child abduction, they mobilized all their resources to pursue the case.

"He's no longer FBI. He owns his own security and investigation business."

She felt a wave of relief wash over her. Maybe he was acquainted with the other agents, and they could join forces instead of feeling isolated like she and JD had been. "What's his name?"

"Jesse Hamilton."

Chapter Twenty-One

THE EXCHANGE BETWEEN JD and Cassie maintained a sense of unease during the journey. JD was aware that Cassie carried concerns about their upcoming wedding, but for him, his son commanded one hundred percent of his focus. Nothing else held significance in that moment.

He vowed to make it up to her once they located Henry Kyle and ensured Vivian St. Amant was behind bars. JD was astonished that the older woman had resorted to such extreme measures.

Then, a sudden thought jolted him like a lightning bolt: What if the FBI demanded a paternity test? In his heart, Henry Kyle was his son, a bond that transcended DNA. But the lingering doubt gnawed at him—what if Vince had been right and Henry Kyle wasn't JD's biological son? The mere idea of them tearing Henry Kyle away from his familiar surroundings and loving home clawed at JD's heart.

He swung open the door to stretch his legs. He felt an urgency to continue this journey after responding to her inquiries.

"Is Jesse meeting us in Oxford?"

"He's already there on vacation with some of his family. His dad—Senator Blake—owns a home there." In this pursuit, that had been the most fortunate aspect. Jesse could act swiftly on any leads, outpacing their efforts. It wouldn't be long before they located his son.

With indifference spreading across his face, he chose to depart the Jeep. "I'll pump. Why don't you get us some drinks and snacks?"

Cassie nodded in agreement and walked purposefully toward the convenience store, her footsteps echoing on the pavement.

As JD gazed at her, he couldn't help but feel overwhelming gratitude for having her in his life. It dawned on him that he needed to end pushing her away. After all, Henry Kyle would soon be her son, and she already cherished him as if he were her own.

The gas tank was full, prompting JD to enter the convenience store. As they stood in line to make their purchases, Cassie nodded and smiled uncertainly.

JD's confident stride faltered as he realized the impact of his actions on her, making her feel uncertain in his presence. He knew he had to repair the damage but had pressing matters. He informed Cassie that he needed to use the facilities.

As he stood in the restroom, the jarring sound of his phone pierced the silence. Fearing it might be Henry Kyle, he fumbled to grab it with one hand, narrowly avoiding dropping it into the urinal. To his dismay, it was the FBI on the line. He hesitated to answer, knowing they would likely reprimand him for pursuing leads without their approval. They didn't know he had sought outside assistance, which would undoubtedly ruffle their feathers when they found out.

As JD hurriedly splashed water on his face with one hand, he quickly exited the restroom and caught sight of Cassie waiting by the Jeep. Just as he was about to open the exit door, something captured his interest, prompting him to halt and pivot on his heel.

He was in a hurry and didn't have time to pick out big, beautiful bouquets, but he knew he needed to make amends. With no time to spare, he hastily grabbed the humblest, pitiful bouquet available and quickly proceeded to check out.

As they stood next to the Jeep, JD handed Cassie a pathetic bouquet, a bright smile lighting up his face. "I'm sorry," he said.

She accepted the flowers and took a sniff of the blossoms. "For what? You've got nothing to be sorry for."

"I've been an ass, and I'm sorry. I'm so wrapped up in finding my son. I can't think of anything else." He moved closer and rubbed her soft cheek, then her bottom lip. "I promise you. After this is over, we'll have that wedding."

As she turned away from him, he felt a sharp pang in his chest. She smiled at him before settling into the Jeep's driver's seat. "Then let's hit the road."

His heart swelled with an overwhelming sense of joy and contentment as he journeyed to locate his son and unite his family.

As he approached the passenger side of the car, the jarring ring of his phone disrupted the quiet. Fumbling with his pants pocket to retrieve it, JD let out a frustrated curse. The limitation of having only one functioning arm irked him to no end.

"Have you found him yet?" He decided to take a proactive approach before they could inquire about his activities.

"Not yet. We've got the Oxford field office working on the case, so when she arrives, we're ready." Agent Miles exuded a sense of calm confidence and control, a striking departure from her former partner, Nick Angler, whose reckless actions had jeopardized the lives of Cassie and her friend.

"Let me know when you do." JD finished the call, a sense of inevitability tugging at him as he was sure the phone would ring again. And indeed, it did.

"What now?" He considered the pleasantries to be finished.

"Where are you, Mr. Walker?" Agent Miles asked.

Considering that it was his son, he felt there was no justification for deceiving the FBI. "I'm not quite sure. But I'm probably closer to Oxford than you are."

Agent Miles sighed loudly into the phone. "I know this is your son, and you want to be there for him. But please let us handle this. You've been in law enforcement. You know civilians can really muck up our work."

Muck up? Was that her way of expressing frustration without using profanity? JD wanted to laugh. "I got it." After ending the call, he made a mental note to follow up with the FBI once he had gathered more information from

Jesse. He was relying on Jesse to work well with the Oxford FBI team.

He settled in the passenger's seat and sighed. Cassie quickly glanced in his direction before returning her attention to the road. "Agent Miles?"

"Yes." JD's throat tightened as he fought to keep his composure. He was determined not to allow the FBI to ask for a paternity test.

"Don't worry. We'll find him." Cassie maneuvered her car past an 18-wheeler, then smoothly merged into the adjacent lane, demonstrating her adherence to at least some of the traffic laws.

He knew he couldn't put it off any longer. Sitting across from her, he felt the weight of his concerns pressing down on him. It was necessary to have this conversation if they were to move forward with their marriage plans and a life together. JD rubbed a hand over his face, trying to gather the courage to address the issues weighing heavily on his mind.

"What?" Cassie's unwavering concern for him always provided a sense of grounding. It signified that he was not facing his challenges alone.

"What if the FBI wants me to take a paternity test before they return Henry Kyle?" She had heard Vince tell him that Henry Kyle might not be his biological child but Vince's. Despite the uncertainty, he had always considered Henry Kyle as his son and had chosen not to delve into the truth, especially after Vince had passed away.

"How about we cross that bridge if it happens? Let's focus on getting Henry Kyle back first. Leave the other thoughts—including the wedding—for another day."

JD thought it good in theory, but he couldn't shake off the persistent fear that consumed his thoughts. The thought of losing Henry Kyle was simply unbearable.

Chapter Twenty-Two

I BREATHED A sigh of relief as I thought about how I had just replaced the license plate on my car, a decision that may have saved me from a potential traffic stop. I couldn't help but notice a highway patrol car following me for what felt like an eternity, but then it suddenly turned off with its lights flashing. It struck me odd that they didn't stop the car before that call, but I'm choosing to focus on my good fortune rather than their incompetence.

As we approach Oxford, I find myself in a state of uncertainty regarding our next steps. I had everything meticulously planned, but complications arose due to JD and the FBI interfering sooner than expected. I am confident that they have the Memphis airport under tight surveillance, which leaves me questioning whether Henry Kyle would be willing to cooperate with so many people around. It's clear that I need to reassess our available options.

As I pull into the Ole Miss Motel, I am greeted by a quaint establishment with a maximum of a dozen rooms.

Vince spoke fondly of this hidden gem, reminiscing when he and Susan would escape to this peaceful retreat. The mere thought of Susan brings back a flood of memories and emotions.

If the woman weren't already dead, I'd kill her for lying all those years about Henry Kyle. Why hadn't she chosen my son? He had more wealth and better looks, and overall, he was a better choice than JD.

I find it essential to let go of any lingering negative thoughts about things beyond my control and instead direct all my energy toward persuading Henry Kyle that he is my grandson and Vince's child. Henry Kyle's intense loyalty to JD needs to be redirected.

As Henry Kyle remains in a deep slumber, I deftly slip out of the car to complete the check-in process at the motel. I fervently hope that this will mark the final instance where I must administer medication to him. My supply of drugs is rapidly dwindling, and I am desperate for him to believe in and eagerly embrace the prospect of joining me in our new home, wherever that may be.

Returning to my car, frustration boiled over, and I let out a string of curses. It had been exhausting to persuade the clerk to accept cash for the room. After fabricating a heart-wrenching tale about fleeing from an abusive husband, he finally relented. What an asshole.

As I open my car door, a sinking feeling washes over me. Henry Kyle is nowhere to be found. I desperately scan the surroundings, but there's no sign of him. Frustrated, I slam the car door and call, "Henry Kyle, where are you?" The sound of my voice echoes unanswered.

After threatening the clerk with my gun, he allows me to view the parking lot security tapes. Henry Kyle pretended to be asleep as I registered at the motel office. I watched as he silently slipped out of the vehicle.

Son of a bitch! Now what?

****

Seeing that Cassie was tired, JD offered to take over driving for a while.

"With your broken arm? No thanks."

Her Jeep still had a manual transmission, a rarity in modern cars. With his left arm broken, he would struggle to maintain control of the steering wheel while attempting to shift gears, but it could be accomplished.

He glanced at the display as his cell phone rang before deciding to answer. With the FBI at the other end, he knew it wasn't the right time to pick up. However, when Levi's name flashed on the screen, he quickly accepted the call. "Yeah," he grunted in response to his unperturbed coworker.

"Put me on speaker."

JD did so to refrain from relaying the message to Cassie.

"I finally got access to her car's GPS."

Thank the fuck for that. It had taken a long time.

"She was at the Ole Miss Motel in Oxford at—" He recited the address.

Cassie nodded. "I know where it is. We stayed there when LSU played Ole Miss one year."

After being separated from Cassie for so many years, he couldn't help but wonder if he would ever uncover the secrets of her past.

"Thanks, Levi." JD ended the call.

"Um, what if he had more? He did say she 'was' there."

Fuck. He pressed the call button to dial Levi's number.

Levi huffed a sigh. "Thank you."

"Sorry, Levi," JD responded.

"Anyhow, I called the motel for you. A woman fitting her description did get a room by paying cash. She later held the clerk at gunpoint to show her the parking lot footage. It seems a kid fitting Henry Kyle's description exited her car and ran."

JD's heart raced in his chest, thumping so loudly that he could almost hear it. His throat constricted, making it hard to swallow as he tried to calm his nerves. "Did she catch him?"

"The clerk doesn't think so, but she hightailed it out of there fast before the cops arrived, and a search ensued for Henry Kyle."

"And?" JD despised prolonging things. He solemnly promised never to subject a client to such waiting and uncertainty repeatedly. The anguish of anticipation and hope was too much to bear.

"They've got him."

JD closed his eyes in a moment of overwhelming relief and joy as he received the news that his son had been found alive.

"The police chief attempted to contact you, but you must've been in a dead cell area."

Yes, not long ago, they had passed that point in their journey. "Anything else? Did they find her?"

"No, they haven't found her yet."

Cassie looked at her GPS. "We're about to exit onto Highway 6, about forty minutes from the motel. Where did they take Henry Kyle?"

Levi relayed an additional address and phone number for JD to dial. "Is that all?" JD refused to conclude the call until he had gathered all the details.

"That's it. Go get your boy." Levi ended the call.

Euphoria gushed through JD. Finally, his son was safe. He dialed the number Levi provided.

"Oxford Police Department."

"Yes, this is JD Walker. I believe you have my son, Henry Kyle."

"One moment, Mr. Walker."

JD was astounded by the remarkable resourcefulness displayed by his son in managing to outwit his captor and break free from captivity. Knowing Henry Kyle's exceptional intelligence and imaginative nature, JD couldn't help but marvel at his son's ingenuity. Nonetheless, he found it somewhat unexpected that Henry Kyle had waited as long as he did before making his move until he recollected that Henry Kyle had managed to make a crucial phone call.

"Mr. Walker, this is Chief Crawford. I'm here with Henry Kyle."

Thank the fuck. "Thank you, Chief. Is he okay?"

"He's a smart boy. He hid until he spotted us and raced to us for help."

"May I speak with him?"

"Sure thing."

"Dad?" Henry Kyle's voice broke on the one word.

JD's stomach churned as he felt a surge of emotions rise. The thought of what could have happened made him feel sick to his core, but at that moment, he was on the phone with his son, who had managed to escape abduction. A sense of overwhelming pride washed over him. "Hey, champ. How are you?" He immediately realized it was a senseless question, given the circumstances.

"I'm good. Are you coming to get me?"

Henry Kyle's voice resonated with strength, but an underlying worry tinged his words. "Of course. We're about thirty minutes away. Can you wait that long?"

With a weary-sounding sigh, Henry Kyle responded, "Yeah. They're nice here."

"Are you hurt?" Please don't let that woman have injured him.

"No. They checked me out since she kept drugging me, but the paramedics said I was okay. I didn't want to go to the hospital without you."

Drugging him? That devious bitch! It was clear that she believed that sedating him was the only way to get his son to cooperate. "We'll see what you need when we get there. Let me talk to Chief Crawford again. I love you."

"Love you, too, Dad."

"Yeah, Mr. Walker?"

"Are you searching for her?" He didn't have to specify who the "her" was. They all knew by now.

"Yes, but we're not having any luck. In case she's run, we've expanded the bolo north and south of here, but nothing yet."

"Just keep my son safe. Please. And Chief–"

"Yeah?"

"–thank you." After ending the call, JD strongly desired his son to be with him immediately, not in thirty or forty minutes.

Cassie glanced at him with concern. "How is he?"

"He's good."

"What about Mrs. St. Amant? Did they catch her?"

JD shook his head, a shiver running down his spine as a sense of foreboding washed over him, knowing that the woman was still out there, evading capture. "No."

"What do you want to do?"

"We're going to my son. My friends will find the bitch who stole him away."

JD called Jesse Hamilton to provide the latest information and instruct him to go after Mrs. St. Amant.

Chapter Twenty-Three

JD'S URGENT LEAP from the Jeep was entirely understandable before Cassie had even fully parked. Her fierce determination to confirm Henry Kyle's safety transformed her into a frantic, protective figure. It made her question her unexpected parental instinct.

Was this how it truly felt to be a parent? The constant worry…the relentless anxiety…the gut-wrenching pain? Was she truly prepared for such a heavy responsibility? Before today, she'd have confidently responded "yes" without a second thought. However, despite her concerns, she managed to maintain a composed demeanor due to having to address JD's mental and physical health issues at the same time. Yet her heart couldn't help but keep Henry Kyle's well-being at the forefront of her thoughts.

As she grappled with the thought of being Henry Kyle's parent, she pondered if she was ready for the responsibility. A sense of unease gnawed at her, creating an emptiness within. The weight of providing the best care for Henry Kyle and her self-doubt burdened her shoulders, making her feel weighed down.

Cassie released her seat belt and reached the police headquarters door. She didn't dash as JD had done.

A professionally dressed woman with graying hair met her when she entered the brightly lit station. "Right this way, Ms. McKay."

A heart-wrenching scene struck her as she was escorted to the chief's office. JD's grip on Henry Kyle was firm as tears streamed down his worn, haggard face. The weight of emotion in the room was palpable, with every nuance of JD's expression revealing a complex mix of sorrow and concern.

Cassie struggled to recollect the last instance she had witnessed JD shedding tears. She questioned whether it had ever even occurred. Her heart bled for him and this long-awaited reunion, yet she couldn't shake the feeling that her emotions were somehow detached. While she experienced the gut-wrenching anguish of Henry Kyle's abduction, it seemed to pale in comparison to JD's deep despair. She pondered whether she had masked her pain by immersing herself in other thoughts. Alternatively, she wondered if she had subconsciously placed JD's well-being above all else, including his son's welfare.

Henry Kyle squeezed out of his father's hold. "What happened to your arm?" He pointed at the sling and cast on JD's left arm. Before JD could answer, the youth turned to her.

"Miss Cassie!"

Henry Kyle dashed towards her with urgency. As Cassie opened her arms to embrace him, she was nearly swept off her feet by Henry Kyle's swift and forceful movement. The warmth of the hug enveloped her, mending the emotional wounds she had been carrying. She held Henry Kyle even tighter with closed eyes, finding solace in knowing he was safe. She couldn't help but think of him as her boy, a sudden realization contradicting her previous conclusion about not being ready for parenthood because she hadn't experienced the same level of concern as JD. Yet, as she delved deeper into her thoughts, she acknowledged that her worries mirrored JDs, albeit differently. While JD was entirely focused on locating his son, she pondered whether she had used that distraction as a temporary respite for JD's mind.

"Henry Kyle." Her heart fluttered and twisted as if it had shattered and then been meticulously pieced back together by the gentle touch of his hand. That touch affirmed his unharmed, secure, and whole being. Tears cascaded down her face, marking the profound realization of experiencing parental love. She hadn't brought this boy into the world, but she knew that losing him would be akin to a violent ripping out of her heart and soul. "I'm so glad you're safe."

Henry Kyle wrapped his arms tightly around her as if she cherished a special place in his heart. She couldn't help but wonder if he would ever come to see her as a motherly figure. It was a thought that lingered in her mind, something she hoped they could navigate together after the wedding.

Pushing away, Henry Kyle smiled. "You and Dad don't need to cry. I'm fine. That crazy lady may have drugged me, but I figured it out and faked it later so I could get away from her. Did you hear that I escaped? I pretended to be asleep and ran when she entered the building. Then, the police showed up, and I went to them.

Did they tell you that she said I was her grandson? She was a major crackpot."

Cassie was sure that he hadn't breathed during that speech. Her mind was fixated on the possibility that he had been drugged. She glanced over Henry Kyle's head at JD, who was watching them with a peculiar look. She couldn't figure out the look or dwell on it now. Had they taken Henry Kyle to the hospital and had him checked out? Was he okay? Would there be any lasting effects from the drugs?

"JD," she said, her voice filled with concern, "do you think we should take him to the hospital?"

JD turned to the chief.

The pair's appearance must have raised curiosity in the man. Their faces were marked with cuts and bruises from the shattering glass, and JD had a broken arm. It seemed necessary to disclose the details of the accident to him, as failing to do so might lead to unnecessary worry about a potential domestic incident, given the bruises on her arm, neck, and chest.

The chief paused momentarily, glancing back and forth between her and JD. "That wouldn't be a bad idea. We had an EMT check him out, but he refused to go to the hospital until you were here."

With a determined look, the confident man took purposeful strides forward and reached out his hand. "Hi, I'm Chief Butch Crawford. You must be this Cassie I've heard so much about."

As Cassie shook his hand, she turned wide-eyed to Henry Kyle. She couldn't help but wonder that he had spoken about her to this stranger. Her curiosity was overwhelming, but she knew she couldn't ask. "Thank you for saving Henry Kyle for us," she said, trying to hide her unease.

"It was our luck and pleasure. Now," He took a step backward, his eyes shifting between them as they closed ranks on Henry Kyle. "We have a lot to discuss, but getting this boy checked out is more important."

Cassie contemplated whether JD had informed Chief Crawford about their joint efforts with HIS to locate the kidnapper. She suspected that he hadn't found the opportunity to do so yet, especially considering the circumstances surrounding his entrance into the station. He might have intended to broach the topic before tears occurred.

She had reached a point where she no longer cared if the chief found out. JD assured her that Jesse and his team would apprehend Mrs. St. Amant, and she trusted JD's words. It was clear that JD had become cautious about trusting others, especially after enduring numerous betrayals over the past year or so.

"Tell you what–" Chief Crawford said with a county boy's drawl as he grabbed a ballcap labeled "Police Chief." "–I'll drive you over, and we can chat along the way. We still need Henry Kyle's full story. He's been so full of spit and vinegar; we've hardly caught a word he's said."

Cassie giggled while JD comforted Henry Kyle. Henry Kyle, however, became tense. "Spit and vinegar? What is that?" He turned curious eyes to his father. "Have you heard that before, Dad?"

JD shook his head with a broad grin. "No, but we are in North Mississippi now. Just like we say certain sayings, they do also. That's probably one of them."

"Well," the chief drug out the word. "It's actually something else and vinegar, but we have a woman present, so I'll keep it like it is."

Cassie had heard the expression "piss and vinegar" and knew JD had also heard it, yet she had never understood it.

"What?" Henry Kyle asked.

Chief Crawford ruffled Henry Kyle's hair. "Don't you worry none."

Henry Kyle ran his fingers through his messy hair, his frustration evident in his attempts to fix it. Cassie observed the tension in his movements, knowing he despised this gesture. She hesitated to intervene, aware that the police chief was not one to be told what to do.

As Chief Crawford uttered, "Let's go," he strode confidently towards the waiting dark police SUV. JD gallantly offered the front seat to Cassie, although she sensed his strong desire to sit beside his son in the backseat. She imagined JD's unwavering gaze on Henry Kyle for the foreseeable future. Despite her reluctance to avert my eyes from him, Cassie had no choice but to comply.

As the chief securely fastened his seatbelt, he steered the vehicle out of the parking lot, assuring the others, "The hospital is just a short distance away."

Cassie shifted in her seat, focusing on Henry, Kyle, and JD. Despite JD being a grown adult, she couldn't shake the feeling that she was somehow responsible for both. Still….

"So," Chief Crawford said, "we got that she drugged him with something in the water she gave him, even made him drink it along the way, but we don't know how he avoided it the last time to remain alert."

Cassie was drawn to Henry Kyle, almost leaping out of his seat in her peripheral vision. With eager anticipation, the boy leaned forward between the front seats.

"I pretended to sleep longer than I actually was so she wouldn't make me drink the water anymore. I guess I fooled her because she let me pretend-sleep."

"That a boy," JD said with pride evident in his voice. "That was brilliant of you to realize what was happening."

Henry Kyle looked back at JD with the same proud smile as his father and spoke. "Yeah, but she shot someone when I called you." He jerked back to the front. "Chief, did someone check on the man I told you about? Is he okay? I'd hate to think he died because of me."

Despite being abducted, drugged, and taken on a road trip, this remarkable kid showed immense concern for a total stranger's well-being. His maturity beyond his years filled her with the same pride she'd seen on their faces.

Chief Crawford turned in the seat to speak with Henry Kyle. "He's okay, buddy. Just a little wound, and he'll be right as rain."

Cassie couldn't help but overhear Henry Kyle's boisterous whisper to JD. "Is that another one of those sayings?" She couldn't suppress her smile as she fought to contain the laughter welling up inside her. It was clear to her that Henry was in for a surprise if the sayings took him by surprise, considering the diverse staff at the hospital, each with their unique expressions and idioms.

As JD and Henry Kyle exchanged hushed words, she turned to the chief with a concerned expression. "Do you have any leads on Mrs. St. Amant? I heard she left before you arrived," she inquired, her voice tinged with worry.

After shaking his head, Chief Crawford frowned and said, "We missed her and don't have her location. Based on the video surveillance at the motel, we put out an APB on the vehicle she was driving, but we think she's either changed cars or is holed up somewhere." He reassured her, "Don't worry, though. We'll get her."

Cassie crossed her arms tightly over her chest, her expression giving off an air of skepticism. *Famous last words*, she thought.

Chapter Twenty-Four

AS THEY ENTERED the quiet emergency room, Chief Crawford guided JD and his family to the khaki-colored, cloth-covered chairs near the intake desk. JD's protective instincts kicked in, knowing that Mrs. St. Amant was still out there and that he had not disclosed everything to the FBI. JD's fear was evident, harking back to the time he was shot while cradling a toddler, Henry Kyle.

Chief Crawford returned to them, his weathered features furrowed with concern, and removed his ballcap, slapping it against his pants leg. With a sense of urgency in his voice, he explained, "They'll take him back in a minute because drugs can disappear from the system rather quickly. We need to know what she used as evidence in her criminal trial."

Criminal trial, my ass. JD anxiously contemplated whether she could escape if he caught up to her. Massaging his throbbing head with his good hand, he tried to push the disturbing thought out of his mind. Clearly, she needed mental help after losing everything when Vince was killed, a tragedy that he couldn't help but feel responsible for, even though it wasn't entirely his fault.

She'd joined the loony bin. She had already proven to be capable of harming a total stranger to ensure that she could keep his son by her side. What would she be willing to do to someone like him if he dared to stand in her way?

JD rose from his seat and expressed his gratitude, saying, "Thanks, Chief Crawford," as he reached out to shake the lawman's hand. Although JD felt the urge to embrace the man for returning his son, he resisted, letting that unmanly feeling pass without action.

"Butch, please," the lawman said, clasping hands, the unspoken understanding of fatherhood passing between them. "After he's done, swing by the precinct so we can try to coax a lucid statement out of him." Butch looked down at Henry Kyle, who appeared as the cat who ate the canary. The boy's cheeks were flushed, his eyes wide and filled with desperation.

"We'll do that," JD offered with the first genuine smile he had felt since the discussion of their wedding with Cassie. He glanced at her. He knew he had deeply hurt her feelings. But even now, he found it difficult to focus on their upcoming marriage and suspected she felt the same way. Perhaps her enthusiasm was just a facade to divert his attention. However, he didn't want to be distracted and say everything wrong.

"Now," Butch said, "do you need me to direct you to a place to stay? I'm sure you won't want to drive back tonight, especially with the FBI on their way to my office to meet us when you're done."

JD was grateful that the chief had persuaded the local FBI to let him and Cassie spend time with Henry Kyle at the hospital without being disturbed by agents. He swallowed hard, trying to push down the lump in his throat. "Thanks again for holding them back. I know you need to play nice with them—"

Butch waved away his last words. "Don't you worry none about my relationship with the bureau. You worry about when the other ones catch up to you." Butch slapped him on the back. "I'll see you later." He turned. "Bye, Miss Cassie. Bye, Henry Kyle. I'll see you later."

Henry Kyle sprang to his feet, pausing momentarily with an uncertain look. Eventually, he reached out his hand. "Thank you, Chief Crawford. Please extend my thanks to everyone."

JD felt a surge of pride as he observed his son. He was growing up so quickly. Despite still being a boy, being surrounded by adults had accelerated his maturity in a way that J.D. found challenging to accept.

A woman wearing a broad smile and light pink scrubs gracefully approached them. "Chief, are we ready?"

"Martha, I'm going to leave you with these fine folks. I've got a few hotheaded alphabets to head off at the pass." He nodded and turned to the exit.

The nurse tsked. "That man is always battling with one or the other from the federal building." She turned back to Henry Kyle, smiling. "You must be our new patient. Are you and your parents ready to go back?"

"Oh," Henry Kyle said, "she's not my mom. She's my dad's girlfriend. Well, they are getting married, but they aren't now. I guess that'll make her my mom, then." He turned to his father. "Won't it, Dad?"

His son was a bundle of excitement and nerves, often causing him to chatter rapidly and incoherently.

"We'll worry about that later, champ," his father reassured him.

In his peripheral vision, JD noticed Cassie tense up. Damn, he'd done it again. He'd put his foot in his mouth. He'd make it right later.

"We're ready," he told Martha. He extended his hand to Cassie, but she rose to her feet unassisted. The anguish he had inflicted upon her weighed heavily on his heart. He mentally recited his priorities: *Check out Henry Kyle...get the feds out of his life without a paternity test..., and then he'd do whatever it took to bring Cassie back around.*

"Maybe I should wait out here."

Cassie's words cut through him like a knife. Despite not being legally married, they were a family, and he refused to let anyone, especially a deranged woman, tear them apart. "Don't be ridiculous," he reassured her as he gently took her hand. "Let's go."

As they followed Nurse Martha through the "Do Not Enter" sign, they entered the bright, sterile space of the emergency room. The overwhelming whiteness made JD's eyes ache, and he felt a wave of nausea and a pounding headache, likely a result of both his injury and the stress of the day. Despite considering getting medical attention, he ultimately decided against it. He was unwilling to take the chance of ending up in the hospital once more, leaving him unable to protect his son from the deranged woman.

After making sure Henry Kyle was comfortable in a curtained area and on the bed, JD and Cassie stood by as a male nurse carefully inserted a needle to draw blood from their son.

"Now," the nurse was telling Henry Kyle, "as brave as you are, I bet those puny ole drugs disintegrated on sight."

Henry Kyle giggled. "No. They made me sleep."

The nurse glanced at him and observed the blood flowing into the tube. "So, they did, huh?" He looked down again, carefully replacing a full tube with another. How many tubes of blood were they drawing? His son was not big enough for them to drain him to death.

When JD was about to express that sentiment, the nurse removed the rubber band from Henry Kyle's upper arm.

The nurse carefully withdrew the needle from Henry Kyle's vein and applied gentle pressure with a cotton ball. After properly disposing of the needle, he secured the cotton ball and Henry's elbow with tape. "There you go, champ. All done," the nurse reassured.

"Hey. My dad calls me 'champ,' too."

JD noticed the nurse wearing a nametag that displayed his name. Lee offered a warm smile to JD, then turned to Henry Kyle and remarked, "He sounds like a smart dad."

Henry Kyle nodded so hard JD's head hurt. "He's the smartest man I know."

Lee ruffled Henry Kyle's hair, which his son flinched, ducked, and reshaped to a godawful style. It was high time to take his son to the barbershop for a much-needed haircut—he was determined to ensure Miss Patricia's scissors would no longer be involved in shaping Henry Kyle's hair.

JD's vision suddenly became unfocused, the surroundings blurring as if he were looking through frosted glass. He struggled to maintain his balance, swaying slightly as he tried to regain his composure.

Cassie's voice was filled with concern as she looked at him. "JD, are you okay?"

He closed his eyes, feeling a wave of dizziness wash over him. Despite the sensation, he refused to acknowledge it. "I feel better now. It was just a momentary lapse," he assured her.

"Maybe we should have you checked out. You haven't even been out of a coma a full day yet. And, health-wise, you shouldn't have left the hospital when you did."

"You were in a coma?" Henry Kyle inquired with surprise, lacing his voice. "Really? What was it like?"

As Lee narrowed his eyes at him, JD sensed trouble coming. Quickly, he put up his hands and exclaimed, "Oh no."

"Oh, yes," Lee, with a concerned expression, said to JD, "Please, have a seat. Let me look at you," as he retrieved a narrow pen light and gently waved it over JD's eyes.

JD adamantly claimed, "I'm fine," yet his words fell on deaf ears as no one would acknowledge his assurance.

Henry Kyle leaped off the bed. "Here, Dad. Maybe you should sit down. You look kind of funny."

Cassie's gentle touch on his back worked like magic, coaxing him to agree to get it over with reluctantly. Despite the lingering headache, he felt a sense of relief and newfound resolve, knowing it was only momentary.

"Okay, but we're wasting Lee's time."

"It's my time to waste. Now have a seat."

JD stepped forward and sensed the impending pitch. A wave of dizziness overwhelmed him, causing him to fall to the floor before grabbing the table. After composing himself, he reassured them, "I'm okay. I just slipped."

Lee pulled back the curtain and called out to someone passing by. Suddenly, a large man in hospital scrubs hoisted Jesse off the floor.

After brushing off his pants, JD coolly remarked, "See? I'm perfectly fine."

"I'm Dr. Habeeb," the big brute said. "I disagree. Sit on the table."

JD reluctantly consented to the man's request and sat at the table. However, as the moments passed, a wave of dizziness engulfed him, compelling him to recline and rest.

"He's got swelling on the brain from an accident," Cassie informed him.

Turncoat, he thought.

No matter how much he pleaded and reasoned, his words were ignored. In no time, he found himself confined to a sterile hospital room, a place he dreaded being. The looming anticipation of imminent tests added to his unease. Having his loved ones, Cassie and Henry Kyle, by his side provided some comfort, but he couldn't help feeling apprehensive about what might come next if the hospital decided to extend his stay after the tests and results.

As he waited, he reached for his phone to reply to a text message. It was comforting to know that someone was there for him.

Cassie ended a call and turned back to him. "That was Chief Crawford. He said you owe him big time for keeping the feds from storming the place to get to you and Henry Kyle."

JD was confident that he did. It must have been quite challenging, particularly in a small town.

"Mr. Walker?"

Jesse lifted his gaze from his phone and noticed a young man standing before him, holding a wheelchair. JD let out a low growl. "You don't seriously expect me to be using that contraption to get to my tests, do you?"

"Well, yes, I do. And you'll need to put on a hospital gown."

Unacceptable. "I'm done here." He rose from the bed, feeling unsteady as he swayed slightly.

Cassie was at his side immediately. "JD, look at me."

He did. "I'm not going through this right now. I just got Henry Kyle back."

She nodded. "I get that, but think of it this way. If you don't, we must meet with the FBI. Look at Henry Kyle. He's sleeping. Do you want to bring it all back up to him right now? That's the first non-drugged sleep he's had this day. Do the tests. Let him rest, and I'll watch over him for you until it's time to battle with the feds."

He always found her reasoning reassuring and cherished that quality in her. She was always right. He entrusted her with caring for his son, who looked serene while peacefully sleeping in the chair beside the window.

JD sighed. "Okay. But–" he raised his voice, "–I'm not wearing a hospital gown."

The orderly turned, leaving a hospital gown on the wheelchair. "I wouldn't let Dr. Habeeb hear you say that."

Even JD didn't want to engage with the imposing man. He couldn't help but wonder why Dr. Habeeb had chosen to pursue a medical career instead of professional wrestling. JD was convinced he would have effortlessly excelled in the ring, commanding attention and respect with his physical prowess.

"I'll be back in a few minutes. I expect you in the chair—*in* a hospital gown."

JD had been making a concerted effort to rein in his penchant for swearing, but the stress of his current environment was causing his frustration to boil over. He knew he needed to maintain his composure. As he grappled with the situation, he realized he still hadn't formulated a response for when the FBI inevitably inquired about Mrs. St. Amant's motivations for kidnapping Henry Kyle and falsely claiming him as her grandchild without any evidence to support her claim.

As JD carefully inspected the gown that Cassie had brought to him from the wheelchair, the door to the room quietly opened, causing him to look up in anticipation.

"Thank God. There you are. Get me the hell out of here. No one here will listen."

With his hands held high in a gesture of surrender, Jesse Hamilton entered the room with a broad grin spread across his face. He was closely followed by a man sporting a distinctive cowboy hat. "Sorry, buddy. You're on your own with that."

Chapter Twenty-Five

AS THEY ANXIOUSLY waited for JD's scan results, they found themselves in the company of Jesse and a man known as "Cowboy." His nickname's origin remained a mystery, shrouded in the sights and sounds of a classic cowboy—from the iconic hat to the unmistakable Texas drawl. Despite the intrigue surrounding Cowboy, JD had to set aside his curiosity and focus on more immediate concerns.

"I'm sorry to bother your vacation," JD said. "I had no idea you were here already, but I'll take that piece of good luck."

Jesse turned to Cowboy and grinned. "He's the one you should apologize to. We're here for his wedding."

"Oh shit. I'm sorry, man." He had already jeopardized his chance at a successful marriage. He didn't want to do the same to a stranger. "Please, do your wedding. We'll get along fine without your help."

Cowboy tipped his hat back and brought it down with a sharp slap against his denim-clad thigh. "It's all right. We've got a couple of days. To be honest, the women were getting on my nerves. I needed the break."

Jesse laughed as he spoke, "That's an understatement."

"I just need something to blow up, and I'll be fine."

Cowboy shocked JD with those words. Blow something up? Now, he was more intrigued by this cowboy. *Later. Focus on Mrs. St. Amant.*

"It's not just the two of you, is it?" He anxiously wished for a larger team of men to be available to track down the elusive woman. JD was determined that no one would miss the wedding, especially Jesse and his team.

Laughing, Jesse shook his head. "Not on your life. The whole family and most of the teams are here."

"Teams? As in more than one?"

"I'm up to three now, bud. We've got a lot to catch up on. When the time is right. Now, let's talk about your problem."

JD glanced at Henry Kyle, who was now wide awake and staring at the men.

Cassie, noticing Henry Kyle, appeared to comprehend the predicament. "Henry Kyle, would you like to come with me to grab something to drink from the cafeteria for everyone?"

As he gazed at his father, the apprehension in Henry Kyle's expression triggered an overwhelming urge in JD to leap from the bed and envelop his son in a comforting embrace. "It's okay. It'll only be a minute, champ. You're safe here." He shifted his gaze to Jesse, who met his eyes and nodded almost imperceptibly. At that moment, JD felt a surge of gratitude towards Jesse for his foresight in bringing along additional men.

"Henry Kyle, I'm Jesse, and this ornery cuss is Cowboy. Outside the door are some of my men who will be with you while you're in the hospital. Is it okay if they come with you to the cafeteria?"

Once again, Henry Kyle glanced over at his dad. A smile spread across JD's face, prompting his son to nod in acknowledgment before saying, "It's a pleasure to meet you. Thank you for ensuring our safety by having these men here to protect us."

JD couldn't help but notice that he had said "us," not "me," and his heart sank. What terrible threat had that deranged woman used against his son? "Henry Kyle, would you get us a few bottles of water? And see if the men outside want something to drink also."

"Sure, Dad." Henry Kyle hurried out the door after Cassie. JD caught sight of them pausing to converse with someone out of view.

JD felt unease as he contemplated trusting these unfamiliar men, but he had no choice. Trusting Jesse's men was his only option, as he could not take any action himself. "They'll take care of him, won't they?" As the door closed, he kept a steady gaze, seeking reassurance before his son disappeared from view.

"We've got you and your family. Don't worry."

As soon as the door clicked shut, JD slid to the edge of the bed, the tension in the room growing palpable. "Fetch my clothes for me. I intend to leave as soon as the doctor returns."

Cowboy reached for JD's clothing on the hanger on the bathroom door.

Jesse asked with concern laced in his words, "Is that wise? You said you'd been in a car accident recently."

He had kept some of his injuries hidden from him, particularly the swelling on his noggin. Although the injury to his left arm was noticeable, he had chosen not to disclose the full extent of his injuries. "I'm all right. I only did it to ease the concerns of my son and fiancée."

It had been much easier for him to undress with Cassie's assistance. He now faced the daunting task alone, as he wouldn't dare ask one of the men around him for help. Frustrated, he forcefully removed the sling and then struggled to pull up his pants with his left hand. As he did, sharp pain coursed through his fingers and arm, shooting up to his shoulder. *Son of a—*

"Do you need help?" Jesse asked.

JD glanced up, a growl escaping him as he made it clear he wouldn't allow just anyone to help him dress. Unless the person helping was a healthcare worker, he wouldn't accept their help. JD was adamant about not wanting to appear weak in front of his friend and guest. "I've got it," he insisted, though he struggled to get his shirt on. But as he grappled with the fabric, he suddenly realized that someone was quietly rendering his refused assistance. *Damn Jesse.* Yet, he never would have gotten the thing on with his wounded arm.

"Thanks," he grumbled.

Jesse stepped back and nodded as if nothing had occurred despite JD's instructions not to intervene. It strengthened his confidence in this man's ability to safeguard his family and uncover the threat against them.

JD reached for the sling, but struggling with only one functional hand, he found it impossible to thread the strap through the loop. He made a mental note to ask Cassie for help when she returned, knowing that he needed the sling to alleviate the discomfort and pressure on his broken arm and previously dislocated shoulder.

"Before Henry Kyle returns, tell me where you are with Mrs. St. Amant."

With his rugged demeanor, the cowboy casually stepped back against the bright, white wall. He crossed his arms, the black T-shirt stretching along his broad chest. *Blow something up, indeed,* JD thought to himself. It was a wry comment, laden with the implications of a past life spent in the military, dealing with explosives and ordinance. JD mentally shook his head as he tried to push the cowboy's enigmatic presence to the back of his mind. *Stop fretting over the cowboy,* he chided himself. *He's not important in the scheme of things.*

"Devon—my brother—has been pulling traffic cams to check for her and monitor the police communications."

"Can he do that?" JD pondered how Levi procured items for them when he was present. These items, JD suspected, fell into a morally ambiguous or even illegal territory for an ordinary person. However, Levi's employment with the FBI meant he had the means to navigate through such situations.

Cowboy laughed. "Don't matter none. He does it anywho. Damn spook." He mumbled the last two words, but JD caught them.

JD arched his eyebrow quizzically as he glanced at Jesse, who responded with a chuckle.

"Don't ask something you can't handle the answer to."

"Fair enough," JD said. "Has he found her? I'm guessing not if you brought men for my family."

"No luck yet. But we're not resting on this one. We think"—he cleared his throat—"that she'll try again."

JD had arrived at the same conclusion, so he hesitated to let Henry Kyle out of sight. "Yeah, I kind of figure that."

"Don't worry. When we find her, we'll be ready to suit up and capture her. In the meantime, I'd like to leave a team with your family as bodyguards."

Bodyguards? JD couldn't help but wonder when his life had come to needing such protection. He nodded in acknowledgment. He didn't think the FBI would offer such a service, but he needed extra help to watch his loved ones. "Thanks. I'll figure out a way to pay you." He wondered about the cost. He had used most of his savings to buy the house, but he would manage. He always did.

Jesse shook his head. "No need. Consider this one of our pro-bono cases we accept each year."

JD knew that charity wasn't something anyone enjoyed, but at that moment, he couldn't afford to concern himself with the financial aspect of the situation. "Thanks, man."

"Now—" Jesse started before the door opened, and a large, lab-coated man entered the room.

"Dr. Habeeb," JD said.

The doctor looked JD over and raised a bushy eyebrow. "Going somewhere?"

"Yeah, home as soon as we get this over with."

"Really, now?" Dr. Habeeb said.

Jesse and Cowboy moved and laughed. "We'll chat once you're done with the FBI. Come by the house. My men can bring you there."

JD looked at his friend's retreating back. "Chickenshit."

Jesse waved his middle finger over his shoulder as he exited the room.

"No, was it really necessary to remove the sling?"

With a heavy sigh, JD asked, "What'd you find?"

"Are you sure you want to know? It might change your plans."

Fuck me. He nonchalantly disregarded the fact that he had let out a curse. Despite being aware that he was not in full health, the doctor's delivery made it seem even more severe than anticipated. He was relieved Cassie and Henry Kyle were not in the room to witness the distressing news.

"Out with it before my family returns."

"The swelling led to cerebrospinal fluid in your brain. It's not severe—yet. We need to discuss the possible implementation of a shunt as a therapeutic intervention for the management of your hydrocephalus should it continue."

The situation required him to spend more time at the hospital. He could only leave once he was confident Henry Kyle was out of danger. "Sorry, Doc. I can't do this now."

"Hmm. If you don't take prompt action, you'll regress to your previous state."

"How much time do you think?" JD inquired, pondering the duration of Jesse and his team's stay in Oxford to safeguard his family. Would they remain after the wedding? They would have to if the doctor's worries were indeed grave.

"Not enough."

Chapter Twenty-Six

CASSIE'S HEART POUNDED in her chest as unease washed over her. As she stepped back into the room, she couldn't ignore the heavy silence between JD and the doctor. With each passing moment, her worry for JD grew, looming over her like an impending storm.

"Hi, Dad. Where are Mr. Jesse and Mr. Cowboy?" Henry Kyle asked with bottles of water in his hands.

"They had to leave, champ."

"Well," Dr. Habeeb said, "I guess that's my cue to sign your release papers. Call me, Mr. Walker."

As the doctor left, he paused at the open door as if he had something important to say. However, he seemed to change his mind, shook his head, and left without a word. What was he about to reveal?

"JD?" she asked. "Is everything okay? How were the test results?"

Then, her fear shot through her spine as JD flashed that deceptive smile he used while lying on an assignment and said, "Fine."

Knowing that JD probably didn't want to discuss the matter before Henry Kyle, she offered a warm smile and decided to let it go—at least for the moment. She made a silent promise to herself not to leave the room the next time he met with a doctor. Despite not being his wife yet, she felt sure it would happen soon, or at least hoped so. They hadn't had the opportunity to discuss their future plans due to Henry Kyle's return. She hadn't expected to have this conversation now, but the situation was what it was.

JD stepped up to Cassie and lightly kissed her on the lips. "Thank you for keeping him safe."

"Oh, that wasn't me. It's those two outside."

"What are their names?" JD asked.

Cassie took a moment to recall the names she'd only just learned. "Romeo and Casper."

JD nodded and stepped forward, his hand outstretched as he gently reached for hers. "Well, I'm thankful, anyhow." He turned to his son. "Henry Kyle, you ready to meet with the FBI?"

Cassie fixed her gaze on Henry Kyle, her heart sinking as she observed the lump slowly descending his throat. He was clearly frightened, and she couldn't bear to see him in such distress. She couldn't understand why he was so scared, apart from the fact that someone was trying to separate him from his father.

"What will they do to me?" Henry Kyle asked with worry evident in every syllable he uttered.

JD cocked his head at his son. "Nothing, champ. You did nothing wrong."

"But I got in the car with her at camp, and I know I wasn't supposed to do that."

Cassie sighed in relief, feeling the tension in her shoulders ease slightly. She knew the situation would be a simple fix if JD avoided putting his foot in his mouth.

He released her hand and stepped to his son. "Champ, the FBI doesn't care about that. That's between you and me, and I believe you've learned your lesson."

"Oh." Henry Kyle stuffed his hands in his pockets. "So, I'm not in trouble?"

JD touched him on the shoulder. "No, champ, you're not in trouble."

"Good. But what will the FBI want?"

"They'll just want to hear your story. That's all. They'll ask a lot of questions—stupid ones generally."

That got a smile out of his son.

"They'll have you repeat things, so don't get frustrated when they do."

Henry Kyle nodded. "Okay. But why do they do that? Don't they take notes?"

JD chuckled. "They do take notes. And I think they do it because they can." He shrugged. "Who knows with the FBI?" He winked at Cassie.

As a former police detective, JD understood the significance of repeating questions. Sometimes, the victim recalls new information. However, the FBI operated in its customary manner.

"Are you ready?" he asked Henry Kyle.

Henry Kyle adjusted his posture as if about to enter a job interview. His expression exuded a distinct air of seriousness. "Yes, Dad."

"Relax, champ. I'll be there with you the entire time."

Cassie felt a wave of nausea as her stomach churned in response to the situation unfolding before her. It wasn't both with Henry Kyle, just JD. An internal shake of her head indicated her disbelief. It seemed inevitable that it would just be JD, given his role as the parent.

Her mind grappled with a troubling possibility: What if the FBI requested JD to undergo a DNA test? She couldn't predict his response. All she knew for sure was that JD's love for the boy, regardless of biological ties, was unwavering. The mere thought of losing Henry Kyle again would be unbearable for him.

JD led them out of the room, introducing himself to the men who would be following them in the near future. Cassie felt uneasy at the idea of someone coming after Henry Kyle again and was determined to fight tooth and nail to keep the boy safe.

After a brief, tense discussion with Romeo and Casper, JD finally relented and allowed Cassie and Henry Kyle to leave the room. As they left, one man walked ahead while another kept a close watch from behind. The entire situation felt so surreal that Cassie couldn't help but question whether it was all just a dream.

As she settled into the backseat of the HIS men's rental car, she couldn't help but notice JD's uncertain steps. Alarm bells went off in her mind—something was definitely not right. She seemed to need to keep a vigilant eye on the stubborn and determined man.

"Police station or FBI office?" Romeo asked.

"Police station. Butch is keeping the FBI on ice for us. Of course, that's only giving time for our favorite FBI agents to arrive."

Agents Miles and her new partner. Cassie didn't dislike the woman, and she didn't know her new partner. It was something about the FBI vibe Agent Miles gave off. Cassie had been with the FBI but not as a field agent.

Her ex-husband was a field agent, and he emitted the same obnoxious vibe of superiority. Maybe the local agents were down-to-earth like the police chief. Somehow, she doubted it unless they were born here, but she could hope.

As they left the hospital parking lot, the ride went surprisingly fast, and within minutes, they were arriving at the station. The bustling scene indicated a shift change, with a multitude of people and police cars present. Among them, she spotted the county sheriff's SUV in the lot, which made her hope they weren't there for them. Henry Kyle was already visibly nervous, and additional witnesses would only exacerbate the situation.

With hers and JD's hands clasped, they quietly entered the busy station in the same precession as they had left the hospital. She wasn't sure she could get used to being sandwiched between these two men. Wow. That didn't come out right in her mind at all.

Chief Crawford emerged from his office and welcomed them as they approached the entrance. "You look like you've been run over by a truck, JD."

"Thanks, Butch. That's awfully kind of you to say."

The chief chuckled. "I believe in honesty. Now, I'm guessing you haven't eaten." He turned to Henry Kyle. "What about you, son? Are you hungry?"

Henry Kyle nodded. "Starving."

Cassie was aware that the child was frequently famished. After all, he was a growing boy.

"Okay, I'll order some latte dinner, and you can eat while chatting with the FBI."

Cassie cleared her throat. "I saw the sheriff's SUV out front. Are we expecting one more?"

Shaking his head, Chief Crawford tightened his lips. "No. Jurisdiction on another case. Don't you worry none. He's not interested in this case. He's had enough of the FBI to last a lifetime."

Cassie suspected there was a backstory, but she knew it wasn't the right time to inquire. "Good."

JD looked down at her and smiled. "Good catch."

She shrugged nonchalantly. "You've always said a PI must be observant."

"And they should." JD turned back to the chief. "Show us the way."

JD released her hand and then wrapped his arm around Henry Kyle's shoulder with a comforting gesture. "Remember, champ. You can ask for a break at any time. You can talk to me. You can ask questions but don't expect them to answer them. Just be honest, and it'll be fine."

Henry Kyle nodded. His eyes were wide. "Okay."

Cassie's heart bled for the boy. "Chief, where can I wait?"

"Wait?" JD asked. "You're coming with us."

In that fleeting moment, a surge of certainty washed over her, assuring her that everything was finally in perfect harmony between them.

Chapter Twenty-Seven

JD FELT PRIDE as he observed his son's poised demeanor while interacting with the FBI. Though there were a couple of moments when JD became tense, Special Agent Miles remained patient and amicable overall.

"Henry Kyle," Special Agent Miles said, "why don't you let Miss McKay take you to the breakroom for a snack? I want a moment with your father."

"Am I in trouble?"

JD's son's sudden change in demeanor made him want to leap across the table and strangle the woman. Why did she have to scare the boy? "It's okay, champ. It's general police stuff. Stuff you don't have to worry about. You've earned a break, so be happy and take it."

Henry Kyle nodded uncertainly. "Sure, Dad. Miss Cassie, are you coming?" His son stood up from his seat and extended his arm toward the door. He swung it open with a creak and turned, speaking in a not-so-subtle tone that carried through the room, "Those two guys are still there."

JD smiled fondly as he watched his son's unsuccessful attempt at whispering. It was clear that the boy was referring to the HIS men. "It's okay. We're going with them to Mr. Jesse's home."

"Does he have a pool?" Henry Kyle asked hopefully.

"He sure does, and he has a daughter about your age."

Henry Kyle made a sad, disappointed face. "But I don't have any swim trunks with me."

Without any belongings with him, JD's son was unprepared. JD had requested Jesse to arrange for someone to shop for them all, hoping they would remember to buy swim trunks. Just to be safe, JD picked up his phone. "I'll have them pick you up some. Now go." He turned to Cassie, who followed his son. "Thank you."

She smiled and nodded. "Come on, Henry Kyle. I could use some coffee."

"Yuck. I don't know how you drink that stuff."

Grinning at his son, JD swiftly texted Jesse to ask for a pair of swim trunks. He then slipped his phone back into his pocket.

"First," JD said to Agent Miles, "thank you for being so good with my son. Second, thank you for chasing them all over to get him to safety."

Special Agent Miranda Miles nodded. "You're welcome, but we need to discuss your behavior, not your son's."

Despite anticipating it, he made a preemptive effort to avoid a lengthy lecture. "I know. I needed to find my son. Me. I felt like it was my fault he was taken."

She quickly grasped the significance of those few words, and JD berated himself for his slip-up. "Why do you think that?"

Lying his ass off, he said, "Because I sent him to the camp without doing my due diligence on its background."

"Hmm." She wrote something on her notepad.

He disliked her actions. Luckily, she didn't do that with Henry Kyle. JD understood. She doubted him, and she was right. He massaged his throbbing head. How much longer could he resist seeking medical help? How much longer could he remain strong for his son and Cassie?

"Tell me, Mr. Walker. Why does Mrs. St. Amant think she's Henry Kyle's grandmother? That is what she told him."

His heart felt as though a sharp blade had pierced it, causing an indescribable pain. However, the emotional burden of the forthcoming answer weighed even heavier on him, and he let out a heavy sigh. "She thinks Henry Kyle is her son's child."

She arched a perfectly sculpted eyebrow, focused on him. "Is he?"

Rising abruptly from his seat, he struck the table with force before letting out a thunderous roar. "No! He's mine." JD closed his eyes, taking a moment to compose himself before opening them with resolve.

As he sat, he realized the importance of maintaining control. Agent Miles scrutinized his behaviors, facial expressions, and verbal responses. It was imperative that he didn't lose his composure once again. "Look, she lost everything and wants something to hold onto. I'm unsure why she wants to think Henry Kyle is Vince's son, but he's mine and Susan's. I can assure you of that."

"Hmm." She wrote again on her notepad.

How many years would he spend in jail for attempting to strangle an FBI agent? He had never harbored violent tendencies toward women, but she had been testing his limits.

"Look. All I want is for you to catch her so we're safe." Jesse and the team would certainly ensure the safety of his son and fiancée, especially if he had to return to the hospital, but it was his responsibility.

"You think your accidents are her fault?"

Accidents? The woman had lost her mind. Those "accidents" were direct attempts on his life. "Yes. Who else?"

"It's not a secret you've made some enemies during your two careers."

She was right, but still…. "Come on, Agent Miles. You believe these coincidences are connected, so give it up. Mrs. St. Amant wanted me out of the way to have Henry Kyle to herself."

"Would you consent to a paternity test?"

His stomach twisted in knots at the mention of those two hurtful words. Would they compel him to take one? Was it even a possibility? He desperately needed a trustworthy lawyer who wouldn't stab him in the back. "Why would I? Henry Kyle wasn't Vince's son. Susan and I were together when she got pregnant."

"And there's no chance she cheated on you with Vince?"

Bitch. That's what she'd become. Her behavior had never been this troubling before. She had always seemed indifferent and polite, unlike the way she is acting now.

"Look, Mr. Walker, we're just trying to get to the bottom of her behavior. Only a negative paternity test will change her mind if she's convinced Henry Kyle is her grandson."

"The woman has gone over the Loonie bend. I don't think anything will change her mind. She needs psychiatric care, not a piece of paper. She'll say we fabricated it." His vision swam for a moment, and he felt the slight sway.

"Are you okay?" Agent Miles asked, all concerned now.

"I'm fine. I'm just tired and want to be with my son. Are we finished?"

Agent Miles nodded. "For now. Where will you be for the next few days?"

Anticipating the question, he and Jesse had devised a plan. "We'll be staying at Senator Blake Hamilton's mansion." Let her know his potential influence if this situation escalated into a fight.

"We'll be in touch," was all she said to that implied threat. "You're free to go."

Throughout the interview, it was evident that he had been freakin' free to leave. He was not a criminal. As she stood up, he directed a piercing stare at her. "Find this woman."

"We're on it." Of course, she wouldn't commit because they had failed many times, leading to cold cases. JD hoped this wouldn't turn into one.

Exiting through the wooden door of the conference room, JD felt a flood of relief knowing that his son had been taken to join the police chief rather than being led to an interrogation room. As he stepped into the hallway, he caught sight of Cassie and Henry Kyle engaging in a conversation with the police chief. Pausing momentarily, JD observed the trio, noticing how Cassie gently touched

Henry Kyle as if seeking reassurance of his presence. The subtle gesture resonated with JD, evoking his compulsion for tactile reassurance in uncertain situations.

As he moved forward, a sense of relief washed over him, and a faint smile illuminated his face as if the weight of the impending doom of a paternity test had been momentarily lifted. As he approached the trio, he caught a glimpse of Henry Kyle's exhilaration in response to something the chief had uttered. Although the exact words eluded him, the tone conveyed an infectious excitement. Witnessing his son's open display of emotion, unobstructed by fear, filled him with a profound sense of contentment.

Cassie was the first to see him, and she touched Henry Kyle on the shoulder. "Your dad is done," she said.

"Dad, Chief Crawford says the house belongs to a senator. Did you know that?" His excitement was palpable.

JD chuckled at the boy's exuberance. "I did. Are you ready to go?"

"Will I be able to swim tonight?"

It was late, but he imagined there were pool lights. "We'll see. First, we have to say goodnight to Chief Crawford." He turned to the chief and shook hands. "I'm in your debt."

Butch shook his head. "All in a day's work. A good day's work."

"Will you keep me updated?" JD asked.

"If I find out anything from the feds, or we get anything local, I'll let you know. I can't imagine being fearful my son could be stolen away. I won't let you suffer through not having timely answers."

JD nodded his thanks. "Cassie, are you ready?"

"We are. Our protection detail says it's only a few minutes away."

Safeguarded by a protection detail, he couldn't fathom that the necessity of such measures would extend to himself or his beloved ones. Scratch that. He fervently hoped never to find himself in a situation requiring such vigilant protection. "Well, then, let's get a move on." He nodded to Romeo and Casper, and they exited the police station.

Romeo spoke with a slight Southern accent that JD couldn't quite place. Louisiana, maybe? "The women have set up a buffet in case ya still be hungry. They be having rooms ready. And," from the passenger seat, he turned back to Henry Kyle, "Reagan and Amber be waiting to meet ya and go swimming."

"Did they get me swim trunks?"

Romeo nodded. "They sure did."

JD mouthed, "Thank you," Romeo smiled, turned, and readjusted his ballcap. JD would bet that boy was a Southern boy through and through.

"Only girls?" Henry Kyle asked as if they had cooties.

Casper chuckled.

Henry Kyle plopped back and wrapped his arms across his chest. "Girls."

That made everyone laugh, and the heaviness of the entire day temporarily left them.

Chapter Twenty-Eight

AS THE TEAM entered the massive house, JD felt awkward. He suspected the senator needed such a large house to accommodate his big family. This house was more extensive than any other home he had visited, and they had several wealthy clients on the coast.

"Keep your hands to yourself," he told Henry Kyle, worrying his son might accidentally break something JD couldn't afford to replace.

Jesse stepped forward, extending his hand to JD. "Henry Kyle, don't worry. When you see the number and ages of kids around here, you'll understand that we ensure everything is replaceable." His words were a comforting reassurance.

With wide eyes surveying the home, Henry Kyle smiled. "Yes, sir."

Kate moved from beside Jesse. "We have a room set up for you two. Henry Kyle, do you mind sharing a room with our cousin's son, Brandon? He's eleven."

His son's eyes lit up with excitement. "I don't mind at all!" he exclaimed, anticipating the new adventure evident in his voice.

JD bet his exuberant response was because there was a boy around his age, not just girls, as Henry Kyle had fretted.

Kate showed them all to their rooms, where Henry Kyle met Brandon. The boys talked nonstop about stuff JD still hadn't wrapped his head around—anime.

Inside their room, Cassie went to the bed and threw herself down dramatically. "I'm exhausted."

He bet she was after all the driving they'd done that day. He looked at his watch and cringed. It was late. Thank goodness the women had had the foresight to provide food for them.

"Do you think they'll be offended if we just crash?" Cassie asked with her eyes closed.

JD walked over to the neatly packed bag of clothing resting on the bed, feeling gratitude for Jesse's support in ensuring his family's needs were met. "Probably not, but I'd like to go down and catch up on the case."

The silence lingered as he awaited a response, prompting him to shift his gaze toward Cassie. She lay fast asleep, her face marked by the telltale signs of exhaustion. It was clear that she needed rest.

Feeling weary, he longed to accompany her, but he recognized that this moment offered the perfect chance to assess the team's progress in locating the kidnapper. It was evident that Mrs. St. Amant couldn't evade them indefinitely. She was blocked from any travel except the road. And then, they'd be monitoring the last license plate number at tolls and other traffic cameras. Most likely, though, she changed plates or even cars. She had the means to do just about anything.

As he gently kissed Cassie, he felt a rush of warmth spread through him. Quietly closing the door behind him, he made his way downstairs. The excited chatter inside made him smile as he passed his son's room. Despite Henry Kyle's exhaustion, he knew those two might stay up all night.

JD shook his head, his footsteps echoing through the empty hallway as he descended the wooden stairs. The distant murmur of voices drew him forward, and as he finally entered the expansive family room, he was met with the sight of a large group of people. At first, he hesitated, feeling like an intruder in their midst. However, the realization dawned on him that they were not other guests but rather the HIS team.

"Hey, JD. Where's that pretty lady with you?" Cowboy asked in his drawl.

JD felt a surge of indignation at Cowboy's words. Although he acknowledged that she was attractive, how the stranger expressed it made him uncomfortable. "She's asleep," he said, leaving the rest alone.

Jesse stood. "JD, let me introduce you around." As Jesse acknowledged each person, they gave him a nod or wave. "This is my wife, Kate. You've met Cowboy. That's Elizabeth, his fiancée. Her toddler, Ethan, is upstairs." He turned to another set of chairs. "That's Devon and his wife, Rylee." Jesse cleared his throat. "Devon, look up from your computer for a second."

Devon acknowledged the request with a nod and then returned to typing.

JD wanted to laugh but resisted the urge.

"They have two little ones upstairs, Mitch, two, and Theresa, ten months."

Wow, they have a lot of kids for Henry Kyle to play with. He'll even spend time with the young ones. Maybe not the babies, but the toddlers he would.

"There's Jake and his wife, our sister, Emily. Upstairs, they have Amber, who is seven, and Leslie, who is two. Amber and our daughter, Reagan, who is the same age as Henry Kyle, are inseparable and excited to meet him."

The girls his son was worried about. Thank goodness for— What was the kid's name?

"Let's see. You've met Romeo and Casper. This is Lee Walker, our cousin. His son, Brandon, is rooming with Henry Kyle."

Brandon. That's right. Didn't the other guys have real names? Romeo and Casper were funny, but JD didn't feel right calling them by military nicknames after not being a military man himself.

Jesse walked to a beautiful woman. "And this is our sister-in-law, Megan, who has two rugrats upstairs, Ace, who is three, and Pamela, who is eight months. AJ is coming later with the teams. As are the twins and their families."

JD's mind was spinning. The sheer number of people he had to remember was overwhelming. He hoped they would understand if he couldn't recall their names immediately. He knew that more people would be arriving soon, all eager to join the search for Mrs. St. Amant. However, he couldn't help but wonder what they could possibly accomplish here in Oxford.

"Now," Jesse said, changing subjects, "I hope I got the ages right, but expect more people to arrive every day for the wedding. Most will stay here, but some will stay in town at one of the B&Bs."

JD nodded in acknowledgment as Jesse took a seat. He surmised that it was now his turn to speak. "Hello, everyone. I'm sorry for interrupting the wedding prep. I'm thankful for your helping me find the psycho lady who kidnapped my son. I can't rely on just the FBI." Grunts sounded around the room. He guessed they didn't expect to either. "Henry Kyle and my fiancée, Cassie McKay, are upstairs."

He looked around the room and noticed the nods of agreement, which reassured him. Evidently, they cared and didn't seem bothered by the interruption.

"Let's update you on where we are," Jesse said, indicating an armchair for JD to sit in. "Devon?"

Devon looked up from his laptop. "Nothing has hit on traffic cams. I'm still trying to track her route from the motel, hoping that will at least give us a direction to narrow the scope of the roadway. She hasn't used a credit card—at least not one under her name—and no ATM usage. No rentals. There are no other properties in the family's name. Nothing. It's like she disappeared."

"Have you checked the alias she used?" JD asked, disappointed in Devon's summation.

Devon nodded. "I'm running that check also. Nothing on it."

Jesse said, "Chin up, JD. We'll find her." He turned to his men. "Romeo, tell him what you found out at the motel."

JD straightened. Was it something new?

Romeo stood. "Casper and I, we combed the area and spoke with the clerk. It turns out he no be frank with the police and FBI because of his"—Romeo cleared his throat—"other activities."

JD was consumed with finding Mrs. St. Amant before she could involve the FBI and make him take a paternity test. He was determined to prove he was Henry Kyle's father and wouldn't let anyone take that away.

"It no be anything firm, but after she returned to the car and found Henry Kyle gone, she rushed back in to see the cameras, which he wouldn't show her. She kept muttering to herself like a Loonie woman. He thought she must be insane and didn't think much of it. But she mentioned, and he no shared dis with the police, that she'd just kidnap him all over again, and they'd go to Canada."

"Why wouldn't he have shared that?" JD thought it was insignificant.

"He done kept that she come back inside. Of course, they'll see she did when they look at the tapes. But he no want to be involved in a kidnapping, so he acted like he'd never seen Henry Kyle sleeping in the car."

JD didn't see how this made a difference.

"So," Kate said, "we can expect her to try again, which means she's close."

Ah, now he saw where they were going with this line of answers. JD knew the psycho woman would probably try again but hadn't thought about her staying in the area, especially if they did. All he knew was Henry Kyle wasn't leaving the premises until she was captured. He planned to discuss possibly taking time off for Cassie and himself with Gus and Nan. This decision would involve declining new cases, but he was determined to compensate them upon their return.

"How do we catch her?" JD asked, confused about the next step.

Jesse's grim smile told him what he didn't need to hear. "Unless Devon can find an electronic trace of her, we wait."

Although he didn't hear the news he had hoped for, he found solace in the fact that he and his family were in the company of individuals who could shield them from harm. He was grateful for Jesse and his family's presence.

"Now," JD said to lighten the mood, "when is the wedding?"

"We could ask you the same thing," Cowboy said. "When are you hogtying that young lady?"

Elizabeth slapped his chest. "Quit, you brute."

Cowboy grasped her hand and gently kissed it.

JD sighed heavily as if the question pained him. "I have no idea. I'm not even sure we will with Henry Kyle at risk."

At that moment, he heard a gasp coming from the door, and he watched as Cassie turned around and swiftly left.

Son of a— He'd done it again.

Chapter Twenty-Nine

THE TIME FOR games has passed; this is now a full-fledged battle. I am determined to bring Henry Kyle back, no matter the cost. The era of diplomacy has come to an end.

Like a master of disguise, I altered my appearance. Now, I'm a short-haired, fully-gray-haired woman. It's not my usual style as it ages me, but it serves its purpose. The police and FBI were searching for me, but I managed to evade them by checking into a hotel in Memphis, Tennessee. A lucky break occurred when an elderly tour group headed to the casinos arrived early due to a flight cancellation. I smoothly joined the group, and no one suspected a thing.

My plan is unfolding flawlessly. I strategically befriended some of the tour group members, who kindly invited me to join them for the rest of their journey. It took some convincing, but I managed to persuade the driver to allow me to tag along. Unbeknownst to them, I won't actually be joining them on their travels. Instead, I plan to utilize their group as a disguise while staying in town to evade the authorities.

I am brilliant. Before I left, I withdrew most of the money from my bank accounts in case my grandson and I had to flee. I now have enough funds to hire transportation daily to keep an eye on my grandson and the criminal calling himself the boy's father.

Locating them takes me no time. Listen to the bartender and the regulars. They'll discuss anything worthwhile, like the FBI and a missing child case in their backyard. Henry Kyle and his father appeared to be staying at our state senator's home. Luck is on my side. I donated to all the campaigns for Senator Hamilton, so I can possibly use that access.

Well heck. I can't use my name, but that's not a problem. I'll think of an alternative. There is always a way to choose from, especially with so many older adults. I've noticed more than one who would be a good fit. There are quite a few women with—as we call it back home—blue hair.

If everything were perfect, I would work as staff in the senator's home. Unfortunately, Henry Kyle and JD Walker know what I look like, so even with a new hairstyle, I won't be able to fool them. How can I get close to them?

I had the delightful coincidence of finding myself in a tour group comprised entirely of writers. Some were actively working on their writing, while others had been published earlier in their lives. What an ideal situation! I realized that I could take advantage of this and subtly gather inspiration from them, as if I were an author in the midst of writing my next book, without raising any suspicions. I couldn't contain my excitement about this unexpected turn of events.

Their suggestions for my fictitious book are initially impractical because of being known. Nevertheless, I feign interest in considering them. I vanish for a day, ostensibly engrossed in writing, but in truth, I am surveying the senator's residence. Unfortunately, this endeavor turns out to be fruitless as the property is surrounded by towering magnolia trees that obscure any view of the house and its surroundings. This leaves me at a loss.

So, I reappeared to the group and acted as if my story hadn't worked. I use the line that the father and daughter saw my character—I couldn't be too specific in case they heard the local news. The group enjoyed the challenge and dug into new options for my proposed novel. Little did they know they were contributing to a future crime. But, oh well, no one would hold them accountable for their ideas alone. Otherwise, many authors would be in jail for ideas acted upon by criminals.

The only idea that might work is finding someone who works for the senator and blackmailing them or buying them off for information. How to find that person was an idea to decide another time. The group wanted to think about it and enjoy some Memphis entertainment.

I wanted to strangle them all. I know they didn't realize the urgency of the situation. Every minute longer that Henry Kyle was in the hands of JD Walker, it meant he could grow into that faux father and be a murdering, kidnapping criminal when he grew up, and I wouldn't allow that to happen.

I found a driver who had compassion. I shared a story about my son cutting me out of his life and denying access to my only grandson. The driver agreed to drive with me an hour and a half to the senator's house daily. One day, he parked at the end of the street so I could see the driveway. I needed someone to bribe.

On the third day, I hit paydirt. I saw a man leaving the house whom I had seen at the hotel bar one evening. As an older gentleman, he might return, and things could go from there. Flirting is an easy way to learn more about Henry Kyle's situation. Yes, this man would be my target.

As much as I hated it, I had to procure more ammo and maybe another weapon. A stun gun might be a better idea, as I hated shooting that man at the gas station. Nightmares of him coming for me have plagued my sleep. Could I survive another night if I killed someone? If it were the only option, I'd have to take a sleep agent because I will have my grandson with me.

I know if I bring my story to the FBI, they'd make JD take a paternity test, but then I'd be in jail. That would only put Henry Kyle into the foster system, and that was no way for my grandson—my heir—to live. Whoever houses him will use all the money I've saved for him before he comes of age. You can't trust people with lots of money. Greed tends to win over.

At the closest mall, I purchased one of those slinky dresses I hate to see women wear. It was necessary, so I swallowed my pride and wore it to the bar, hoping to find this gentleman. There was a big difference between the skirts and jackets I wore. Money should dress like money, not like sluts. But this dress cost enough—ridiculous prices for clothing in the stores.

I meet with my new friends and receive their praises for my outfit. I want to vomit. It clung to my curves like I was looking for an older sugar daddy. But it was, as I'd already admitted, necessary. I pretend to blush and tell them it was my splurge to up my spirits. That was an easy lie because they knew I was down about my writing.

I walk past the bar where I have seen the gentleman drinking, but he isn't there. I wait patiently at a small table nearby. When he finally arrives, I feel nervous, knowing I'm deep in this situation. This will make it much more serious, but I must do what I can. Right now, though, I'm out of ideas.

So, I slinked to the bar, sat near him, and ordered a drink. The bartender placed my martini before me and went to serve my mark.

"Hey, Bernie. The usual?"

Bernie. I could work with that.

"What's the usual?" I cooed. "Because this martini isn't doing the trick."

Bernie turned to me, looked me up and down, and smiled.

Pig.

"Hi, gorgeous. Why, it's an Old Fashioned. Would you like one?"

Before I could respond, he told the bartender, "Jeff, would you get my lady friend here an Old Fashioned? It seems as if your martini is losing its touch." He laughed.

"Scootch over here." He patted the bar stool next to him. "We can enjoy our drinks and chat. It's not fun drinking alone."

"You've got that right." I pick up my heavy black purse, which has my gun in it and my newly acquired stun gun, and move to the bar stool next to him.

Check. I'll do what it takes to checkmate and access Henry Kyle.

Chapter Thirty

THE STAIRS SEEMED to stretch endlessly as tears blurred Cassie's vision, making each step treacherous. She tripped and caught herself as JD's hurtful words echoed in her mind, causing her heart to ache with every beat. Just a few days ago, they had eagerly planned to marry quickly, and now everything felt uncertain. Henry Kyle's importance was undeniable, but the idea of their marriage being in jeopardy was unbearable, especially since it had been JD's suggestion to marry so quickly.

She felt an urgent need to flee from this place. Despite being engaged to JD, she couldn't escape the nagging suspicion that their engagement was a beautiful illusion, far removed from reality. The looming presence of Vivian St. Amant posed a constant threat to Henry Kyle's safety. She couldn't help but wonder if this was to be her fate—to be kept on the sidelines by JD, much like Susan, without ever becoming his wife.

She was resolute that she would not wait indefinitely for him to marry her. While there was no urgency for an immediate marriage, she insisted that a commitment had to be made at some point. She had dreams of having a family, and she was unwavering in her stance that she would not have children out of wedlock, despite the commonality of such situations among women today.

Cassie felt a sense of urgency and longing for solitude as she went to the bedroom. Once inside, she deliberately closed and locked the door before leaning against it, seeking the physical barrier to symbolize her desire to be alone. At that moment, she couldn't help but wonder whether JD would even consider following her; she concluded that he likely wouldn't bother. This realization stirred up a mix of emotions within her, leaving her to ponder the extent to which he was indifferent to her feelings and how this indifference seemed to benefit him conveniently.

Her emotions were tumultuous, urging her to collapse onto the bed and let her tears flow freely. However, she resisted the impulse and instead reached into the closet, her fingers closing around the clothing the Hamiltons had procured. Determined to give JD space to deal with the complexities surrounding Henry Kyle, she decided to leave. She planned to throw herself into her work, hoping that time would help mend the fractures in her heart.

Wiping the tears from her face, she sniffed and straightened her shoulders. *I can do this.* She grabbed her clothing from the closet and dresser and tossed it haphazardly into the bags they'd been found in earlier. Who cared if they were wrinkled? That was a minor thing to deal with in her life. Next, she went to the bathroom and collected the toiletries Kate had given her. She'd stay at a hotel tonight and fly home tomorrow.

As she contemplated her next steps, she decided to leave JD her beloved Jeep and rent a car to journey to Memphis. She eagerly reached for her phone, using its search engine to find and select the perfect rental option. As she heard the dial tone, a sense of relief washed over her, a glimmer of hope that, finally, something was falling into place for her.

A gentle knock echoed through the room as she stood by the bag of her meager belongings, causing her to pause. Her heart fluttered with anticipation at the possibility of JD coming to talk about their future together. Despite knowing it was a bit irrational, she longed for him to commit to a specific date for their wedding. The uncertainty weighed her, and she craved the reassurance that he was genuinely dedicated to their impending marriage.

"Cassie, it's Kate."

Cassie's heart plummeted as she realized he hadn't mustered the courage to follow her himself; instead, he had sent an emissary. Disappointment and betrayal washed over her as she muttered, "Coward."

Cassie gently brushed away the stray tears from her face and ran her fingers through her messy hair, sighing heavily. After composing herself, she slowly opened the door. "Kate," she said, forcing a cheerful tone, "what's up?"

Kate looked past her to the bed and the bag of personal items and raised an eyebrow. "Got a minute?"

Cassie glanced behind her, realizing her attempt to flee had been poorly concealed. "Sure." She opened the door wider, allowing Kate entrance.

Closing the door behind them, Cassie stood while Kate went to the bed and gingerly sat beside the bag.

"Are you leaving?"

That was obvious, but she'd play the word game. "Yes."

"Why?"

Kate understood the reason, and it frustrated Cassie that she asked her to explain it. "Because JD needs to focus on saving Henry Kyle, he doesn't need someone else to worry about. Besides, cases are backing up at home."

"You know there is a house full of men dedicated to protecting all three of you, so JD doesn't have to worry."

Dang her for making a compelling argument with the truth. "I need to go. That's all."

"It has nothing to do with what JD said about your marrying?"

Cassie scoffed. Of course, it did. "No. I know we have to wait." *Lie.*

"Hmm." Kate looked around the guest room with admiration. "I've always loved this guest room."

Nodding, Cassie agreed. "Yes, it's charming." Why the chitchat now? She narrowed her eyes at Kate. "What are you trying to say?"

Kate's smile faltered. "Sorry. I'm not good at small talk. I guess it shows."

Cassie nodded. "A little."

"We don't want you to leave. JD would be heartbroken if you did."

Cassie shook her head. "I doubt that. He knows I'll be waiting for him at home when he's ready to return." And she probably would with that stubborn heart of hers.

Kate stood. "Are you sure I can't change your mind?"

"No. But I thank you for trying. Maybe another time. Besides, you have a big wedding to plan."

"We do." Kate laughed. "Good luck to you. I hope you'll keep in touch."

Cassie liked Kate and planned to stay in touch after JD and Henry Kyle left the residence. "Sure thing."

They embraced tightly, holding each other briefly before Kate approached the door.

"How are you leaving? Are you taking the Jeep? Do you need a ride? Where are you going?"

Cassie laughed at Kate's rush of questions. "I have a rental on its way. I'll fly out of Memphis tomorrow. I don't have a flight yet, but they have several daily."

Kate nodded. "Okay, then. Good luck."

"Thanks, Kate."

Cassie gently closed the door behind Kate and paused, her hand resting on the doorknob. A wave of uncertainty washed over her. Was she making a mistake? No, staying was definitely the wrong thing to do. JD needed to concentrate on Henry Kyle's safety, and she had to ensure it.

She finished including the final item from the bathroom and dropped the bag to the floor. Making another sweep of the room, she turned and reassured herself. Opening the door to head downstairs and wait outside for her ride, she was startled. JD stood on the threshold.

His pained eyes strayed to the bag in her hand.

She couldn't help but wonder if he still loved her or if she was just convenient to him. The idea of him having to sleep alone weighed heavily on her, but she couldn't shake off the unsettling doubts.

"Going somewhere," he asked in the softest voice she'd ever heard him use.

Once more, she adjusted her posture, drawing herself up and squaring her shoulders. She steeled herself with determination, acknowledging that she could indeed face this situation. Although it didn't constitute a full-fledged breakup, it certainly felt like one. "Yes. I think it's best given the current situation."

"Is it because I've put you in the line of fire with Henry Kyle's kidnapper? Or something else?"

He knew dang well why she was departing alone. "You have enough to worry about. Keep Henry Kyle safe, and I'll keep Gus's business going. When you've caught Mrs. St. Amant, I'll be waiting." *Maybe.*

His fingers threaded through his tousled hair as if trying to unknot his thoughts and messy locks. "Cassie, I don't want you to leave."

She anxiously waited for him to say something more, but all he did was let out a deep sigh. Finally, she found the courage to say the words weighing heavy on her heart. "I want to leave, though," she confessed. As the words escaped her lips, it felt like her heart had been torn in two, but she knew she had to be honest with herself and him.

"Cass—"

"Cassie, your rental is here," Kate shouted from downstairs.

"Rental?" JD asked. "What about your Jeep?"

"I'm leaving it for you and Henry Kyle to return home when this is over."

"Cassie, please."

"Move out of the way, JD. I'll see you when you return home."

Without warning, he made a startling and abrupt movement to allow her to pass. With a heavy heart and a sense of sorrow that weighed her down, she walked past him. Looking back at him, she could not bid him farewell or utter those parting words. Deep down, she was resolute not to say goodbye. They would have to work through their issues when he returned home. It was a challenge they simply had to face together.

As JD stood by without taking action to prevent her, Cassie became confident that their relationship would never be the same again.

Chapter Thirty-One

CASSIE SETTLED INTO line at the historic hotel nestled in the heart of Memphis, Tennessee. She patiently waited to check in and conversed with a group of seasoned travelers. They excitedly shared their plans to visit Biloxi, Mississippi's bustling casinos. Since they had some unexpected free time due to flight cancellations, they decided to make the most of it by embarking on the famous Graceland tour.

Observing their infectious enthusiasm, Cassie couldn't help but marvel at the youthful spirit exuded by these older travelers. Their zest for life and adventure left her hopeful that she and JD would maintain the same vitality as they aged.

JD. Since she and JD reunited, she felt an intense and all-encompassing love for him that seemed to ache in the depths of her heart. Despite being acutely aware of her selfishness, she found it impossible to suppress this overwhelming feeling. While prioritizing Henry Kyle's safety, she believed she and JD could still build a life together. Refusing to be strung along like Henry Kyle's mother, she longed for the sacred union of marriage and dreamt of having children in that precise order. These desires tugged at her heart with a force she couldn't overlook.

His words echoed in her mind, a constant reminder of their uncertain future. *"I'm not even sure we will with Henry Kyle at risk."*

Heck, they may never catch Mrs. St. Amant. Had JD meant that they would never marry if that were the case? That's how she understood it.

Later, slumped in the solitary armchair of her dimly lit hotel room, she let out a deep sigh. Self-doubt began to creep in. Perhaps she should have lingered and engaged him in conversation. Yet, his resolve seemed unyielding, and she could not bear the weight of his rejection. They had endured a lengthy wait and had overcome countless obstacles. Could this be the one that diverted them from their path together?

Cassie felt that she wasn't essential to keeping Henry Kyle safe. She saw herself as just an additional person to monitor, so she believed removing herself from the situation would be best. Feeling resigned, she pulled up a travel app on her phone to arrange a flight home. As predicted by the group, all flights to Gulfport had been canceled due to severe weather in the area. Despite the inconvenience, she managed to secure the next available flight, which was scheduled for departure in two days.

Cassie felt her heart lurch as a sudden knock jolted her from her thoughts. Her hand darted to the grip of the gun nestled in her purse, her mind scrambling through a flurry of potential scenarios. Sudden adrenaline surged through her as her heart pounded fiercely. Could it be JD following her? If only it were that simple.

Approaching the door, she asked, "Who is it?" and peered through the peephole, her heart racing. A head of gray hair came into view, but the tension in the air was unmistakable.

"Mrs. McKay, we're wondering if you'd like to have a drink with us," one of the gray-haired women asked.

The travel group she had encountered in the lobby suddenly caught Cassie's eye. Despite not feeling like socializing, she knew staying cooped up in her room with her sad thoughts was not an option. With a bold decision, she flung open the door and exclaimed, "I'd be delighted to join you for a drink. Let me grab my purse." The unexpected turn of events had piqued her curiosity, and she was eager to see where this evening would lead.

As they walked to the elevator, they reintroduced themselves.

"This," a woman Cassie remembered as Maryse said, "is Joe." She pointed to a tall, rather good-looking older gentleman. "This is Walt." She nodded to the other gentleman. "And these ladies are Ethel and Willa." The two giggled.

"We're twins," one of the ladies said. Cassie had no idea which twin was which, but she didn't want to be rude and ask.

"I see," Cassie said, nodding as she gazed at the two identical figures before her. They looked strikingly similar, from their matching attire to their features. However, she couldn't help but think that leopard-print yoga pants were a bold fashion choice, especially for people their age. "I'm Cassie," she said, reminding them they had referred to her by her last name.

"Great," Maryse said as they entered the elevator. "I hope you have our names down. Because Cassie, you might have to remind us of our names later." The lady winked and smiled, and the group chuckled.

Cassie smiled at the absurdity of the joke. "I'll do my best."

Maryse, the most talkative of the group, addressed her again. "So, what brings you to Memphis?"

"I'm traveling back to Gulf Islands. I'm a PI there."

"Ooh," one of the twins said, "Are you on a case? Can we help? I've always wanted to be a PI."

As Cassie shook her head, a wistful smile tugged at the corners of her lips. She wished she had money for every time someone expressed their desire to become a private investigator. "No case," she replied, recalling the trip to Oxford.

"Oh," the other twin said dejectedly.

Throughout dinner, her companions showed unflagging curiosity, asking her about her cases. Without breaching confidentiality, she divulged brief descriptions of her cases, which satisfied them. Not once did she mention JD by name; she only referred to him as her partner. Despite her efforts, the exclusion stung. The looming question of how they would react upon JD's return weighed heavily on her mind. Would he be relieved that he wasn't heading toward marriage? The mere thought of a potential future without him was gut-wrenching.

Despite being bombarded with questions, Cassie deftly inserted her inquiry. Surprisingly, she learned the group had united online to create a casino travel group. They planned to convene at various locations throughout the year to venture into different states and experience new casinos. This upcoming trip was conveniently located near Cassie's residence, and she eagerly anticipated the opportunity to join the group. There was even a possibility that they would be on the same flight departing from Memphis.

"So," she asked after sipping her Chocolate Martini, "are you all retired?"

"No, dear," Walt said. "We're writers of some sort. Didn't we say that?" He shook his head. "Probably not. Anyhow, that is why we are so interested in your cases. Research, don't ya know." He waggled his eyebrows, and Cassie laughed.

As she reflected on the intense scrutiny they subjected her to, she briefly contemplated her retirement plans. What would she do once she retired? Despite her savings, she realized it would not be sufficient to sustain her. Inspired, she decided to start documenting her cases in a journal, intending to use them as material for future articles or books to generate additional income. It seemed like a promising plan for her future.

"Is it difficult to write?" she asked, then sipped her cocktail.

They all nodded. "It is. Even after years of doing it," Joe said, "it is still difficult getting words on a page unless your muse is active."

Well, that idea of extra income went bye-bye. Maybe she'd learn to bartend.

"Oh," one of the twins said, "you might be able to help Maryse. She's writing about—"

Maryse interrupted her. "Look, there's my friend." She gazed toward the door with adoration. "I'll be right back."

Cassie asked. "How many of you on this trip are there?"

"Twenty-five," Joe said. "Oh, plus an add-on. That makes twenty-six."

As Cassie glanced at her watch, the late hour came into focus, casting a spell of weariness over her. The day had been arduous, and the brief respite at the Hamiltons' was no match for her exhaustion. As she contemplated bidding her hosts farewell, two figures emerged from the shadows behind her. She turned, her heart pulsating with a bewildering blend of astonishment and eager anticipation.

Maryse returned to the table, and Cassie stood.

"Hi, Bernie."

Chapter Thirty-Two

SHIRTLESS, WEARING SHORTS and sunglasses, JD gazed moodily by the pool, only half-watching as Henry Kyle played with the Hamilton children. Every so often, his son would call out, "Dad, look at this!" and JD would feign interest, though his mind was elsewhere. He had really messed up this time. Cassie had walked out on him. It felt like déjà vu from their early days, but this time, he, not his father, had wrecked everything.

A familiar presence loomed over JD, and he knew without looking that it was Jesse Hamilton. The man had an uncanny ability to sense JD's brooding and a steadfast determination not to let him wallow in it, a testament to their enduring friendship.

"Sitting around won't help. We have Henry Kyle, and he's safe. Go after her; it's your best chance."

Oh, how easy that sounded. But…. "Would you if it was Reagan or Jason in danger?"

Dressed similarly, Jesse sat in the lounge chair beside him. "Touché." He propped his feet on the chair. "Devon hasn't found Mrs. St. Amant. This might take a while. Are you willing to risk your relationship with Cassie?"

"Leave it be, Jesse," he whispered, the weight of the decision pressing heavily on his heart. The thought of a life without Cassie and Henry Kyle together was a searing ache. Yet, the idea of leaving his son's safety in the hands of near strangers, no matter how capable, filled him with a deep, conflicting anguish.

"Fine. But Henry Kyle is going to start asking about her. Have you thought of what you are going to tell him? He's been telling Reagan how she will be his new mom."

If it weren't for the children present, he would have aimed a punch straight at Jesse's mouth. "Enough," he gritted out through clenched teeth.

Jesse put his hands behind his head and sighed. "I told the women not to send me, but they thought the message would be best received since we knew each other."

Great. Now, the women were involved. This could be never-ending while he and his son holed away for safety. "Thanks for the help, but no thanks. I've got this."

"That's what I tried to tell them." Jesse shook his head. "You'll learn that these women are incredibly meddlesome, especially when they take a liking to a woman, like they did to Cassie."

A subject change was needed, but JD couldn't keep his mind off Cassie and Henry Kyle.

"So," Jesse said, "Jason is thinking of the Marines instead of college."

Thankfully, a different topic. "How do you feel about that since you've been in the army?"

Jesse took a moment before answering. When he did, he let out a heavy sigh. "I'm okay with it now, but it took me a while to feel this way because I had hoped he would follow in my footsteps. I'm still unsure about him skipping college, but he assures me he will get his degree while in the service, which is entirely possible."

All JD knew was that Henry Kyle was not skipping college, and he hoped his son wouldn't follow in his footsteps. He'd been kicked out of college his first year after destroying the common area of the dorms on a drunken rampage.

"Didn't you tell me he'd had leukemia?"

"That was when he was younger. It's been in remission long enough that he should pass the entrance physical. We'll have to wait and see."

JD shook his head. "I take it that was his argument for the Marines as opposed to college?"

Jesse chuckled. "Yep."

The two of them sat together in comfortable silence, the sound of children playing creating a peaceful backdrop. JD felt a sense of relief that he had reached out to Jesse and that they had chosen to spend time in Oxford. He could see this environment's positive impact on Henry Kyle after the traumatic experience of being kidnapped. Surrounded by supportive friends, Henry Kyle appeared free from lingering side effects.

JD hadn't slept worth shit the night before. All he did was worry about Cassie. Where had she gone? Was she okay? Would she leave him for good, or was this a break so he could focus on Henry Kyle? So many unanswered questions.

He hadn't tried to contact her as he feared her response. His heart couldn't handle losing her forever. Exhausted, he drifted off to sleep in the warm sunlight.

"The wedding is tomorrow. Will he be okay with that?" a soft female voice asked, her worry palpable.

"He'll have to be," Jesse responded, conveying determination and concern. "We won't force him to attend if that's what you mean."

"Of course not," the soft voice replied, filled with understanding. "I just worry it might be too much right now."

The weight of the impending event hung heavy in the air, punctuated by the uncertainty of the situation. JD wasn't sure he could attend, but he also wouldn't be a wuss and shy away.

"Henry Kyle and I will be there," he said without opening his eyes or removing his shades. He stood. "We'll be fine." Then he turned to the house, strode inside, and went to his and Cassie's room.

Children's laughter echoed through the house. In the room his son shared, he could hear the boys giggling. Despite the noise, he felt they had made the right decision by staying put. However, a sense of urgency crept in as he wondered how long he could wait. The longer he delayed chasing Cassie, the more he feared she might doubt his love for her.

But Henry Kyle had to come first. They couldn't remain there forever, and he had to set a limit if the team hadn't developed anything.

A knock on the door sparked a groan in him. He didn't want company, the was why he'd come to his room. "What?" he barked.

"Hey, *couyon*," Romeo said, "ya be wanted downstairs."

JD knew what couyon meant, and he wasn't crazy or stupid. Okay, maybe he was stupid about his love for Cassie and how to show it. "I'll be down in a minute."

"*Merde*. I be trying to bring you down."

Well, heck. He'd given up cursing—as best he could for his kid's sake—but knew a curse word in Cajun French. "Okay, hold on," he said and went to the closet to put on a shirt. He ran his fingers through his hair and decided he looked presentable. When he opened the door, he saw Romeo with a huge smile and felt the urge to slug him.

"The Hamilton women be waiting."

Well hell. He wouldn't have agreed to go downstairs if he'd known that. This had best not be about Cassie. He couldn't stand to hear any more about it. He'd screwed up, and he knew it. He'd fix it as soon as they found Mrs. St. Amant.

As he entered the large family room, he noticed the women and the team. Jesse, Jake, Devon on his laptop, Cowboy, Casper, and Romeo. Who was watching the perimeter?

As if guessing his question, Jesse said, "More of the team arrived and are on duty."

JD nodded. He glanced at the women in the room. "I understand you summoned me. How may I be of assistance?"

That courtesy put smiles on their otherwise grim faces. He'd always known to use honey when things were tense.

"We were wondering," Emily, Jake's wife and the Hamilton baby sister, said, "if you had plans for Henry Kyle's birthday?"

Crap. He'd forgotten his son's birthday with everything going on. JD dropped into a chair and closed his eyes, feeling like his life was falling apart. His gift for his son was at home: a new gaming system he had purchased. It was the one that Henry Kyle had blabbed about nonstop.

With Henry Kyle's birthday and tomorrow's wedding, he wasn't sure what to do about a party. "I hadn't thought that far," he admitted.

Kate nodded. "We thought that might be the case. We want to throw him a birthday party."

"But it's tomorrow and the wedding…." JD couldn't ruin someone's perfect day, but his son did deserve a party. Kids didn't understand when things didn't go normally for them.

"It's okay," Elizabeth, or was it LizzyBeth—Cowboy's fiancée, said. "I don't mind sharing my wedding day with a kids' party. We can have the party in the morning; the wedding is late afternoon. No problem."

"I—" JD started. What could he say? By the looks of everyone in the room, this was a done deal. "Okay," he finally agreed. "I appreciate it. Henry Kyle will appreciate it."

"Great," Rylee, Devon's wife, said. "Ladies, let's see what we have for supplies and make a store run."

"JD, would you like us to pick something up for you to give to Henry Kyle tomorrow?" Kate asked.

He guessed he'd best have something for tomorrow. His present at home could wait until they returned. "Yes, please." He thought for a moment and gave them a small list.

Smiling and chattering nonstop, the women left the room.

"Boy, howdy did you just make their day," Cowboy said. "Those women like nothing more than to plan a party, especially a kids' one."

JD had been wondering something and decided to ask. "Why aren't you marrying at the ranch in Texas? Why here?"

Cowboy shrugged. "That place is busy with guests all the time. We wanted someplace quiet where just the team and a few friends and family would be here."

"Is your family here?"

The cowboy glanced at his watch. "Oh, hell. I'm late." He rushed from the room.

Chuckles bounced around the area. "What?" JD asked.

"He's supposed to pick up his mom at the airport," Jake said. "She's going to be pissed when he's late. She hates to travel to the Memphis airport."

"Who doesn't?" Casper said.

Dang. That boy had blended in the background. No wonder they called him Casper. Ghost he was.

"What now?" JD asked.

"I," Devon said, "keep searching for Mrs. St. Amant. You and Henry Kyle enjoy yourselves. You're safe here."

Enjoy himself? How the hell was he supposed to do that? They were having Henry Kyle's party without Cassie, who had purchased various anime plates, napkins, cups, and decorations. She'd planned a fun affair with the family, Daisy, Gus, and Nan.

JD made a conscious effort to lift his spirits for his son, even though he knew Henry Kyle wouldn't notice the difference. He reminded himself that he and Cassie had overcome similar challenges and were determined to do so again.

Her departure this time left him feeling a profound sense of loss. The road ahead appeared fraught with challenges, far from the ease he had anticipated.

Chapter Thirty-Three

JD SNAPPED AWAKE as the bedroom door swung open. In a split-second reaction, he instinctively reached for his weapon on the nightstand, only to find it missing. Before he could process what was happening, a body leaped onto the bed, and in that instant, he remembered: They were at the Hamilton residence in Oxford.

"Dad! Dad!" Henry Kyle said, bouncing up and down on his knees. "It's my birthday. I'm eleven!"

JD's spirits lifted as his son's excitement bled into him until he realized Cassie had left, not here to celebrate this big day with them.

"Okay, champ. Settle down. Let me wake up a sec."

"But, Dad," Henry Kyle continued but stilled his movements on the bed, "they are having a birthday party for me. Do you think Miss Cassie will be back for it?"

How could he possibly explain this to his son? With a sense of cowardice, he muttered, "I don't know. I'll call her and see."

Anticipation lit Henry Kyle's eyes. "Can you call her now?"

JD closed his eyes. He needed calm and quiet for that conversation—not to mention privacy. "No, champ. It's too early."

"Will you call her before the party, so she has time to get here?"

He would, but she wouldn't be able to return in time if she'd flown back last evening. "Sure. Now, go get dressed and let me do the same. I'll meet you downstairs for breakfast. I bet Mrs. K. will have something good to eat."

"Can we take her home with us? She's a much better cook than you or Miss Cassie."

Henry Kyle giggled, and JD laughed. Tickling his son at the waist, he said, "Boy, don't you let Miss Cassie hear you say that. Now, get."

With agility only for the youth, his son jumped off the bed and raced back out the door, leaving it open. "Brandon, Dad says…" was all he heard as the voice trailed off. He hoped he hadn't alluded to Cassie making it and getting his son's hopes up.

He was infuriated by the thought. Even though Cassie might have ended their relationship, he couldn't fathom how she could disappoint his son on his birthday. Children couldn't comprehend such letdowns, and he was determined to spare his son the heartbreak of her absence.

A shadow appeared in the doorway, and a familiar figure wearing a cowboy hat peeked inside. "Hey, man. I thought I'd tell you I saw your woman in Memphis last night."

Thoughts of hope began to rise within him despite knowing she was no longer *his* woman. Still, he couldn't help but think of ways to win her back.

"She was having dinner with a bunch of older folks, and I happened to overhear them grumbling about their flights being canceled." Cowboy tipped his hat and said, "Just thought I'd give you a heads up." Then he vanished, closing the door behind him.

Putting his hands behind his head, JD let out a heavy sigh. What words could he possibly find to convey his thoughts to her? As he closed his eyes, attempting to form the right words for her, they only seemed to create a chaotic, tangled jumble in his mind.

Maybe the best course of action would be for him to travel to Memphis and meet her face-to-face. However, he had already relied on Jesse for a significant favor involving Cassie, so he hesitated to ask for more during this challenging period; it seemed self-centered. Besides, it would mean taking time away from his son's birthday, and he couldn't allow that to happen.

Picking his watch up from his bedside, he decided to get out of bed and begin the day. Noise from downstairs told him he wasn't the first to wake.

In need of mental clarity and time to carefully choose his words for Cassie, he decided that a brief shower might provide the needed respite. He clung to the hope it would bring him the headspace he desperately sought.

As he stood in front of the mirror, droplets of water cascaded down from his hair, which he vigorously towel-dried. The memory of her leaving filled him with fiery anger whenever it crossed his mind. Yet, amidst the frustration, he realized that his choice of words had led to this situation. Were his words really truthful? Perhaps they seemed accurate in the heat of the moment, but in reality, they were anything but the truth.

Jesse had arranged a small ceremony for JD and Cassie after Cowboy and Elizabeth's wedding. He had wanted to keep it simple and not take away from their big day, so he only asked for a few minutes to exchange vows in front of witnesses. He persuaded Levi and Pat to fly in for the ceremony, but they decided to drive instead due to flight cancellations and would bring the marriage license. Gus and Nan chose not to attend, citing their age and travel as reasons, although he suspected they were actually covering for him and Cassie, who had disappeared abruptly.

What would he tell Levi and Pat now? They would arrive in a few hours. They'd catch part of Henry Kyle's party even though JD hadn't known that then. But it was a win-win, except he didn't have a bride.

After slipping into a new pair of shorts and a T-shirt —not without trouble due to his cast arm—he reached for his phone, intending to call Cassie. However, as he held the phone, he could not bring himself to dial her number. A sense of inertia overcame him, causing him to collapse onto the bed. He rubbed his hand over his weary face and sighed heavily, feeling the weight of his apprehension. He hoped that he could avoid saying something regrettable this time.

He anxiously pressed her name on his call list and waited with bated breath while the phone rang. When voicemail kicked in, he hesitantly ended the call, unsure what message to leave. The worry gnawed at him—had she ignored his call intentionally? Or could it be that she had caught an early morning flight? Trying once more, the result remained unchanged, leaving him with a sense of unease.

This time, he left a message. "Cassie, it's me. We need to talk. I'm an ass. I know it. Please give me a minute to explain. I love you." He ended the call.

As the weight of the situation settled on his shoulders, JD understood that he would soon have to navigate a difficult conversation with his future mother-in-law. He knew he needed to start preparing for an uncomfortable and emotionally challenging discussion about the reasons behind her daughter's absence.

It was fortunate that he had already planned for Henry Kyle to attend public school the following year because he was worried that his relationship with Patricia might come to an end. At least he wouldn't have to see Cassie every morning when he dropped off his son and every evening when he picked him up. He didn't know how he would work alongside her daily. Sadly, he knew that one of them would eventually leave Coastal Investigation.

How could he make such a colossal mess of things?

Chapter Thirty-Four

"HAPPY BIRTHDAY, HENRY Kyle. Happy birthday to you," the group sang off-key and clapped.

With a wide, joyous smile, Henry Kyle effortlessly blew out the candles adorning his anime-themed cake. JD surveyed the vibrant decorations, impressed by the women's effort to capture the exact theme that Henry Kyle had hoped for. It was a bittersweet moment, a pity that Cassie wasn't here to enjoy it with them, and her absence was a stark reminder of the complex family dynamics.

Once again, he was at a crossroads, grappling with conflicting emotions. His heart ached as he struggled to prioritize his son's happiness over his turmoil. However, Cassie held a significant place in his son's life. She was meant to step into the role of his new mother. Or, at least, that was the plan.

JD anxiously dialed Cassie's number multiple times that morning, yearning to speak with her. However, each attempt led to her voicemail, leaving him with the sinking feeling that she intentionally avoided talking to him before her return home.

When his phone vibrated in his pocket, a surge of hope pulsed through him, thinking it might be Cassie calling to give him a chance to explain without further delay. However, looking at the display, he realized it was Levi's number. Panic set in as he realized they must've arrived in town, and he still hadn't figured out how to explain Cassie's absence.

Stepping away from the revelry, he answered his cell. "Yeah, Levi."

"We're pulling up now. Meet us at the front door?"

"Sure thing." He quickly ended the call, hoping to avoid questions or requests for Cassie to take similar action.

Catching Jesse's eye, he nodded to the next room. In it, JD told Jesse about the new arrivals.

"Shit," Jesse said. "What can I do?"

"I don't need anything more than what you already have. This is the dilemma I need to solve."

"Okay, but if you need—"

"If I need to, I'll ask," JD said, then moved to the front door. Jesse nodded and returned to the party.

JD greeted Pat and Levi with relief as he noticed them carrying the birthday presents from his home. He nodded approvingly at the gifts and remarked, "Perfect timing. We're having Henry Kyle's party right now."

Patricia smiled. "Do you think I'd forget my new grandson's birthday?"

Levi corrected her. "He's not your grandson until after tonight, honey."

JD's ears perked up as he tried to process what he had just heard. "Honey?" Had Cassie been right about these two all along? Then, another word caught his attention—grandson. A surge of realization hit him as he prepared to share unfortunate news in that department. "I need to tell you something," he stammered, feeling the weight of the forthcoming conversation.

"Can't it wait, JD?" Patricia asked. "We'd like to see Cassie and Henry Kyle."

JD mentally unleashed every curse word he had vowed never to utter again. "About that—"

"Can it wait until we're at least inside?" Levi asked. It's getting warm out here.

JD hadn't realized he'd kept them on the front porch and in the morning's heat. "Sure."

A glint of movement caught his eye as they turned to the entrance. Turning his head, he noticed another vehicle gracefully navigating its way into the long, winding driveway. A sense of longing tugged at his heart, hoping it was Cassie finally arriving. However, a more profound intuition whispered that it was more likely Cowboy's mom, ready to join the wedding celebrations.

Upon entering, Kate walked up to them. "You must be Patricia and Levi. I've heard quite a bit about you both."

"Good things, I hope." Levi chuckled.

Kate smiled. "All good. Come on back. Henry Kyle is about to open presents."

JD anxiously pleaded with Kate through his gaze, hoping she would understand or agree with him, but she remained unmoved. Despite his silent efforts, she led the couple to the family room and the bustling party. Amid the gathering, Henry Kyle eagerly sprinted to Pat and enveloped her in a warm and affectionate hug.

"Miss Pat," Henry Kyle said, "you made it. Did you bring Miss Cassie with you?"

Pat looked at JD quizzically.

It was now or never to tell her. "She, uh—"

Henry Kyle pointed to the entryway. "There she is."

A sense of foreboding slid down JD's back, and he grabbed his son. "Go finish opening your presents while I speak with Miss Cassie."

Dejected for only a moment, Henry Kyle agreed and sprinted away.

There was something off about Cassie. JD couldn't quite put his finger on it—was she uncomfortable, or was she feeling ill? She hesitated at the entryway, not approaching him or her parents. It felt like she was waiting for him to make the first move, and he would, without hesitation.

As he advanced toward her, he was suddenly frozen in place by a shocking sight: Vivian St. Amant stood behind Cassie, holding a gun to her back. The others noticed the same thing simultaneously as the adults stiffened and reached for their sidearms. However, no one, including JD, pulled their weapons. With children present in the room, there was no way he would allow for an accidental crossfire to harm any of them.

The children, seemingly unaware, continued with the gift unwrapping and laughter.

JD moved closer to Cassie but was too far away to reach her and asked, "What do you want?"

Cassie stood there, her throat working as she swallowed hard. The look in her eyes wasn't one of fear but instead of pain, as if she had just inflicted some deep betrayal.

"You know what I want. I want my grandson," Vivian said from behind Cassie.

"Let us get the children safely out of the room, and we'll discuss this."

She seemed to consider it, glancing around the room. "One of you may take all the children except Henry Kyle out of the room," Vivian dictated.

Henry Kyle, hearing his name, made a beeline for JD. In a display of fierce protectiveness, JD swiftly and firmly positioned his son behind him, shielding the person he cherished most from any possible danger. His commitment to safeguarding at least one of his loved ones was unwavering, and he knew he would address Cassie's predicament only after ensuring his son's safety. "He's not going anywhere with you," he declared, his voice firm.

Chapter Thirty-Five

CASSIE'S VOICE TREMBLED urgently, "You must let the women go also." The realization that Kate and Rylee might be armed hinted at the potential for additional help to protect the children should Vivian seize control of the house.

With a firm push, Vivian guided Cassie further into the room. "Go ahead, but hurry."

Cassie's heart pounded in her chest as the men remained motionless, her anxiety escalating over the fate of the women and children. The method of their selection was a mystery to her, but the sight of Casper and the women, a united front, guiding the remaining children to the back exit brought a glimmer of relief. Despite his unwavering focus on Cassie and Vivian, she knew Casper was watchful, and the children were in capable hands as they were led out of the room.

As soon as the room emptied, the few remaining occupants, in unison, drew their weapons and aimed them in Cassie's direction. The sight made it hard for Cassie to take a breath. Although she trusted the men not to shoot her, she couldn't shake her lack of trust in her captor.

Cassie slowly ran her tongue over her dry lips, her words resonating with tension and resignation. "I pleaded with her to shoot me that I wouldn't bring her here. But instead, she made Bernie restrain me. She spun a story about us taking Henry Kyle from her, and he fell for her deceit."

"It isn't a lie!" Vivian shouted. "You did steal him from me!"

JD raised his hands and slowly separated them, dropping the gun in his grasp to his thumb. "Look, Mrs. St. Amant," he said calmly, "I'm putting down my weapon." Cassie's heart raced as she watched him lean over and carefully place the gun on the floor. She knew that she couldn't let this woman get past her to reach Henry Kyle, not unless she incapacitated or killed her first. She was willing to sacrifice herself to protect that kid.

Cassie stood at a crossroads, meticulously evaluating her options. The tension in the room was palpable, with the men wielding their guns, ready to act. Despite the threat, Cassie hesitated, knowing that she didn't want Henry Kyle to witness any violence, whether it be hers or his father's. Adding to her unease was the worry that Vivian, desperate to salvage her chances of winning, might escalate the conflict by going after JD. At this pivotal moment, Cassie felt the weight of near-certain defeat pressing down on her.

"What are you doing?" Vivian let out a piercing scream as Jesse and Cowboy menacingly closed in on JD. They positioned themselves in a way that allowed JD to move closer to her by shifting Henry Kyle behind them.

"I want my grandson, and I'll leave you be. I'll even let Cassie live."

JD shook his head. "You know we can't do that. Besides, you're a bit outnumbered."

"Yes, but you'll have to go through your precious Cassie to get to me."

While that was true, she didn't worry because several of Jesse's team were sharpshooters and could probably separate the two. But she didn't believe they would attempt a shot if there was a chance of hitting her.

Cassie watched as the entire room closed as a group, shielding Henry Kyle from her view, which meant Vivian couldn't see him. She was going to go more batshit crazier than she already was.

"All it took was for you to take a paternity test, and this would never have come to this."

JD kept his eyes on Cassie as he spoke. "You know I won't do that unless Henry Kyle wants it. He's my son." He paused. "Mine and Cassie's."

Cassie's eyes widened in surprise at his statement. With a mix of uncertainty and hope, she questioned whether he meant now. She felt a surge of affection for this man, a feeling that had blossomed since they first crossed paths in elementary school.

She looked around and assessed the situation with Henry Kyle concealed behind the men. Her heart raced as she contemplated whether she could summon the courage to stand up to Vivian. The thought of potential gunfire from all directions filled her with trepidation, but she knew she had to decide.

"You killed my son to keep your truth," Vivian spat. "Well, it's no longer going to be a secret."

JD inched closer and stopped.

"Henry Kyle," Vivian said, "you come here to your grandmother. It's time we leave."

"Dad?" Henry Kyle asked in a weak and scared voice.

"Don't you worry, Henry Kyle. You're staying where you are. No matter what you hear or what happens, I need you to trust me and stay where you are behind Mr. Jesse and the men. Can you do that for me?"

"Yes, sir."

Cassie's eyelids drifted shut in relief, fully aware of the imminent danger. She braced herself, knowing she had to shield JD from Vivian's second shot, as the first would be intended for her. She could only hope that the impact wouldn't inflict severe harm.

"Cassie," JD said, "I was wondering something."

She drew in her brows. What could he be wondering right now?

"I was wondering if you'd marry me tonight."

His decision left her bewildered. He had clarified that he wouldn't marry her until Henry Kyle was safe. Furthermore, given the situation's urgency, this was the last thing they needed to discuss. They had to focus on bringing this unstable woman under control.

In addition, wasn't Cowboy and Elizabeth getting married this evening? She wouldn't want to intrude on their special day. Furthermore, their spot on the beach held too much significance for her. Feeling an overwhelming sense of sorrow, she shook her head in disbelief. "No, JD."

Not realizing she was saying no to tonight specifically, JD's face fell, and the stress of the past couple of days made him look years older.

"Enough of this," Vivian said. "Bring Henry Kyle to me, or I'll kill her."

Just as Cassie was ready to tell her to "Just do it," she heard— "Try, and the three of us will splay you on this ground."

Upon hearing Casper's voice, Cassie looked in her peripheral and saw Kate, realizing she and Casper, most likely Rylee, had circled the house. Cassie swiftly wrenched herself free from Vivian's desperate grasp. As she did, a searing pain shot through her hip, and the din of multiple guns firing filled the air, intensifying the chaotic and dangerous situation they found themselves in.

Her mind immediately went to Henry Kyle. She surveyed the group and noticed Romeo and Cowboy standing protectively over the boy on the ground. However, her panic shifted to JD, who had been left undefended. Her vision started to blur, making it challenging to focus on him, but his fearful cry was unmistakable.

"Cassie!"

Chapter Thirty-Six

WHILE NESTLED IN her hospital bed, Cassie found comfort with JD by her side and Henry Kyle on the other. She watched Cowboy's wedding on a tablet, unable to shake the regret of not being there in person. Despite the option to postpone the wedding, Cassie had urged them to resume their everyday lives after the morning's events once the police and FBI had completed their rounds of questioning and clearing the scene.

Following a brief surgery, it was determined that the bullet had penetrated through the fatty tissue on Cassie's thigh. Despite the straightforward medical procedure, she continued to experience significant pain. Recovery would take longer than she desired.

"Miss Cassie," Henry Kyle said, "Did you really mean it when you told Dad you wouldn't marry him?"

How on earth could that kid remember that from all the angst of the day? She wondered, her mind swirling with surprise and admiration for Henry Kyle's perceptiveness.

JD cleared his throat. "Champ, why don't you see if Miss Pat and Mr. Levi are here yet?"

Henry Kyle released an exasperated huff, his frustration evident as he declared, "That just means go away so you grown-ups can talk." With that, he turned on his heel and stalked out of the room.

JD took the tablet from her and set it on the tray, rolling it out of the way. He clasped her hand. "You know, he's right. Did you mean it?"

Of course, following Henry Kyle's safety with Vivian in the hospital, JD's perspective on marriage shifted. Initially, he had been reluctant to marry during this time, viewing it as a mere distraction. This reluctance stung, suggesting he had not been wholeheartedly committed to the idea earlier. Although prioritizing Henry Kyle's safety was paramount, the fact that JD had initially hesitated to commit troubled her deeply.

"I find myself hesitating," she said softly, her heart heavy with uncertainty. While her desire to marry him was unwavering, the ease with which he seemed willing to cast aside their relationship at the first sign of trouble troubled her more than she dared to acknowledge. What would happen if another challenging situation arose? She couldn't bear the thought of anything happening to Henry Kyle, but would he again distance himself from her if faced with adversity?

JD dropped her hand, stood, and paced the small room. He ran his fingers through his hair and said, "Christ, I'm sorry, Cassie. I don't know what I was thinking. I can't live without you in my life." He stopped and dropped on the bed again. "We can't live without you in our lives. Henry Kyle and I need you to complete our family."

The words were awe-inspiring, but despite that, she currently couldn't walk down the aisle without the support of a cane or walker. Under these circumstances, she wouldn't consider getting married. "I need time to think about it."

JD sighed, and his shoulders dropped. "I understand." He stood. "Can I get you anything before I leave? Are you in pain?"

She was steadfast in her refusal to take anything that would make her feel groggy. Perhaps they could consider administering a lower dose of painkillers so that she could maintain clarity of thought when contemplating her future.

"I'm fine. I hoped to see my mom before I went back to sleep."

"I'll round her up," JD said as he walked to the door. He halted and shook his head. "I'll be back, Cassie," he said and opened the door.

In a moment of overwhelming emotion, she hurriedly called out, "JD," feeling desperate to stop him from leaving yet unsure of what she would say to make him stay.

He turned with hope in his eyes. "Yeah?"

"Give me an hour." She made a firm decision as she sat in the dimly lit room. She would give herself precisely one hour to feel sorry for herself about her current predicament. After that, she would gather the strength to determine her path forward, whether it would involve JD or not. She was never one to prolong difficult choices, and she wasn't about to start now.

JD nodded and left the room, and the door closed softly behind him.

Cassie closed her eyes and shifted to find a more comfortable position as the effects of the earlier painkillers started to wear off. With a sigh, she reached out and pressed the nurse's button, hoping they could provide her with some aspirin.

Cassie must have drifted into a light doze after the nurse left. When she stirred and reopened her eyes, she found her mother and Levi standing in the room.

"Oh, sorry, honey. We didn't mean to wake you. We were just about to leave you to rest," Patricia said.

Cassie extended her hand and reached for the remote to adjust the bed, gently pleading, "No, stay." Her heart longed to see her mother, yet she felt the weight of indecision pressing down on her. How long had she been asleep? She had assured JD she'd have her decision in an hour.

"I'm sorry you came up here for nothing, but I'm glad you're here," she told her mom. Then turned to Levi. "You too."

"Well, kiddo. We're glad we were here also. Of course, you gave your mother a fright getting shot. Can you not do that again?" he joked with a twinkle in his eyes.

Cassie smiled. "I'll try not to do that again. Too painful," she admitted with a grimace.

"Well, it's late. We were returning to the hotel for the night since visiting hours were almost over." Her mother leaned over and hugged her. "You rest. We'll see you in the morning."

Cassie's heart ached with the desire to cling to her mother, seeking guidance in making this crucial decision about her future. However, she knew all too well that her mother's response would be the same—a simple directive to figure it out on her own.

They left, and a knock sounded on the door.

Cassie panicked. She didn't have an answer for JD. She needed more time.

"Miss Cassie?" said Henry Kyle as he poked his head into the room. "Can I come in?"

"Of course." Cassie looked behind him and noticed he was alone.

"Yeah, Dad was on the phone, so I came back up here. He and Grandpa Gus were talking about work."

"Your father will worry about your disappearance," she said, her voice tinged with fear. She couldn't shake the image of JD's reaction when he found out his son had gone missing again. "You need to go back and let him know you're here," she urgently implored, her concern evident in every word."

"Nah, I told Miss Pat. She'll tell him when he gets off the phone."

Cassie relaxed but didn't like it. "How are you doing?"

"I should be asking you that. You got shot, not me."

Sometimes, she forgot how grown-up Henry Kyle thought. "I'm doing okay. Thanks for asking."

"Okay." He fidgeted, and she knew he wanted to ask something else.

"What is it?"

"Well," he said, "you never answered me about marrying my dad."

Oh no. She hesitated to break the young man's heart, feeling uncertain. She knew she had to have another conversation with JD, reflecting on their relationship and seeking reassurance that he had sincerely and wholeheartedly wanted to marry her right from the start.

"Henry Kyle—"

"I heard he said something he shouldn't have, and that's why you left. I don't know what he said, but I'm going to tell you a secret."

She raised her eyebrows in anticipation. "Go ahead."

"He cried. I peeked into the room and saw him sitting on the edge of the bed, crying. He loves you, Miss Cassie. We both do."

"Yes, we do," JD said from the doorway. "And, young man, you and I must discuss boundaries."

Henry Kyle ducked his head. "Okay, Dad."

"I'm sorry he snuck up here," JD said. "I was—"

"On the phone. He told me. How are Gus, Nan, and Daisy?"

"Good. Daisy's college graduation is this weekend. They're hoping we can make it."

Cassie wanted to attend but was still determining how mobile she would be. "I'll try," she said.

He nodded. "Okay, champ. Please sit in that chair and put on your headphones. And turn them on. We're having an adult conversation here."

Henry Kyle rolled his eyes and did as told.

Cassie's chest tightened under the weight of overwhelming pressure, making it difficult to breathe. Despite the tumultuous time, she knew she had to find it in herself to forgive his lapse of judgment. "JD—"

"Before you speak, Cassie, I want to apologize again. I was a jackass. There was no time that I didn't want to marry you. I couldn't think about a wedding at that time."

"I—"

"As soon as I realized what I'd done, I asked Jesse to hook up a wedding for us so you could see how much I love you, but you left."

"I—"

"But I deserved it. I should have followed you, but I couldn't make myself leave Henry Kyle, and I didn't want to bring him away from protection."

"I—"

"I didn't figure you'd want me to bring the entire HIS family to chase you down. I'm sorry it ended with you getting shot. Christ, if I hadn't run you off, Vivian wouldn't have found you."

"JD, stop."

He closed his mouth and nodded.

"JD, I'm sorry I ran away. I promise never to do it again. I'll marry you if you wait until I can easily walk down the aisle."

"Whoo Hoo!" Henry Kyle said, then turned red being caught eavesdropping.

Cassie mentally echoed the sentiment as JD leaned down and kissed her.

A Note from Sheila

THANK YOU FOR reading *Fractured Trust*! If you enjoyed reading JD and Cassie's story, I would appreciate it if you would help others enjoy this book, too. You can recommend it to friends, readers' groups, and discussion boards. It would mean a great deal to me if you'd take a moment to write a review and share how you feel about my story so others may find my work. Honest reviews help bring my books to the attention of other readers. The best news is that only a few words are needed.

About the Author

SHEILA KELL WRITES about romantic men who leave women's hearts pounding with a happily ever after built on memorable, adrenaline-pumping stories. She is a four-time winner of the Readers' Favorite Book Award for romantic suspense and contemporary romance.

As a Southern girl who has left behind her days with the United States Air Force and as a University Vice President, she can usually be found nestled in South Mississippi, where she lives with her cats and all the strays that magically find her front door. When she isn't writing, you can find Sheila with her nose in a good book, dealing with the woodland critters who enjoy her back porch, or wishing she had a genie to do her bidding.

Ways to connect:

sheilakellbooks.com

facebook.com/sheilakellbooks

goodreads.com/sheilakellbooks

bookbub.com/authors/sheila-kell

I'd love to hear directly from you, too. Please feel free to email me at sheila@sheilakell.com.

Don't miss out on new releases, exclusive excerpts, and giveaways!

Join my newsletter:

www.SheilaKell.com/subscribe

Join my Facebook Reader Group:

www.facebook.com/groups/sheilakellbooks